VOTE FOR McGOVERN

Pandini Towers, the tallest and most splendid building in Kalamazoo City, was lit like a gigantic sparkler against the night sky. The penthouse suite was jammed with Kalamazoo City's movers and shakers. Everyone was dressed to the nines, having paid top dollar to see and be seen, to gawp at the magnificent views of the city from the floor-to-ceiling windows, and above all, to rub elbows with the city's most famous candidate for mayor—Frank Pandini Jr.

Pandini had announced his candidacy not long after Mayor Saunders resigned from office as the

result of the Kalamazoo City Dome scandal. At first it seemed like no one would have a chance against him. He was a celebrity. He was charming. A win was practically in the bag.

But now, with just days remaining until the election, Pandini's campaign was in trouble. His opponent,

District Attorney Patrick McGovern, was running a scrappy grassroots push, convincing many that Pandini's wealth and success put him out of touch with the typical Kalamazoo voter. Of course, McGovern himself was also one of the most prominent faces in Kalamazoo high society—but it wasn't always that way. He grew up in one of the city's poorer areas. And the more McGovern crowed about his own modest upbringing, the more he chipped away at the shine and polish that were the hallmarks of Pandini's brand. Polls showed that Kalamazooans were starting to get the message.

The Pandini campaign needed a shot in the arm.

Pandini was always at his best when he was on the ropes, and this evening was no exception. Surrounded by supporters, encouraged by their generous campaign donations, Pandini beamed. He moved with ease from guest to guest, shaking hands and making jokes.

Irving Myers, Pandini's campaign manager, watched the scene from the sidelines. He needed this evening to be a complete success—and to be the lead story on the Eleven O'Clock Action News.

The waitstaff navigated through the crowds, trays

loaded with small filets of the finest fish, all caught by local fishermen, as well as tiny hot dogs from Frank's Franks, a beloved Kalamazoo City haunt, now owned by Pandini.

Carpy manned the bar, serving up root beer floats, the signature drink of Bamboo, Pandini's five-star nightclub. The bartender had won "KC's Best Drink Slinger" five years running in the *Kalamazoo City Krier* "Best of Kalamazoo City" poll. Everywhere they looked, the guests were reminded of the many ways Frank Pandini Jr. had helped make Kalamazoo City one of the nation's finest.

Myers sidled nervously up to a beefy bodyguard who was eyeballing the crowd, watching for any suspicious activity. "Bobby, our guy has to give the speech of his career tonight," Myers murmured.

"He'll deliver," said Bobby, without taking his eyes off the room. "He's in his element here."

Myers looked beyond the donors to the gorgeous view of the Kalamazoo City skyline. "If he can do that, he's as good as elected."

"For your sake, I hope so," said Bobby with a dark chuckle.

Irving Myers shuddered. He didn't need the reminder. If he didn't deliver a resounding victory to Frank Pandini Jr., he'd be lucky to get hired to run a student council campaign.

Finally, it was show time. The lights dimmed, except for a spotlight trained on the podium placed right before the glimmering KC skyline. Myers stepped to the microphone.

"Thank you all so much for coming out this evening.

I am delighted to introduce to you our next mayor—Mr. Frank Pandini Jr.!"

The crowd cheered wildly as their candidate took the podium. Pandini flashed his signature smile and waved to the crowd while a firing squad of cell phone cameras took photos that would soon be all over the internet. Pandini politely motioned for everyone to settle down.

"Thank you for being here to support my campaign. And welcome to Pandini Towers! Gaze out! We stand atop the highest point in Kalamazoo City." He paused to let that sink in. "And that is where I will continue to take this city—upward!"

Irving Myers smiled as there was even more applause.

"This campaign has taken me to every corner of this city, meeting with citizens and talking with them about their lives, their problems, their hopes and dreams. Let me tell you, without a doubt, this is our country's *greatest* city!"

Pandini paused again as the room filled with cheers.

"You deserve the best leadership, and that is what I will deliver. You know my motto—" He paused yet again to let the crowd chime in:

"YOUR CITY—BETTER!"

Pandini continued, his booming voice filling every crevice of the room. "Better decisions coming out of the mayor's office! Better compassion for the less fortunate among us! Better schools! Better roads! Better opportunities!"

"YOU LIE!" shouted a voice from the back.

Derek Dougherty and the Action News team turned their cameras toward the heckler, whose face was

covered by a ski mask and who, to everyone's horror, held a boomerang above his head.

With hysterical shrieks, the crowd dropped to the floor. Bobby leaped to put himself between the weapon and Pandini. But before he could, the boomerang zoomed through the still air, grazing the candidate's left shoulder, shattering the window behind him, and spraying the floor with glass shards that sparkled in the spotlight. The attacker ran for the podium, unfurling a banner that read "QUIT—OR ELSE!" then leaped out through the broken window, taking flight and disappearing into the night.

Welcome to the campaign trail in Kalamazoo City.

5

Jarrett J. Krosoczka

PLATYPUS POLICE SQUAD

LAST PANDA STANDING

WALDEN POND PRESS
An Imprint of HarperCollins*Publishers*

Walden Pond Press is an imprint of HarperCollins Publishers.
Walden Pond Press and the skipping stone logo are trademarks and registered trademarks of Walden Media, LLC.

Platypus Police Squad: Last Panda Standing

Library of Congress Control Number: 2014949451
ISBN 978-0-06-207168-2

---

15 16 17 18 19 CG/RRDH 10 9 8 7 6 5 4 3 2 1
❖
First Edition

FOR ROBBY AND EMMA

KALAMAZOO CITY WEST SIDE, 9:15 P.M.

Steering the unmarked squad car that was like his second home, Detective Corey O'Malley turned onto Parkside Avenue. As usual, his partner, Detective Rick Zengo, sat in the passenger seat. The partners were working a rare night shift, taking a call about a petty theft on the west side of town. It was a simple assignment—nail some punk teenagers who had been caught on camera multiple times shoplifting backpacks from the mall.

"You hear Plazinski is bringing in a new detective to the team?" O'Malley asked as he brought the car to a stop in the neighborhood where the perps lived. "A 'special investigator,'" he said, making air quotes.

"'Special investigator'?" Zengo replied. "Tell me more."

"All I know is what I overhear in the break room," said O'Malley as he lifted a pair of binoculars to his eyes. "So, not much of much. Some guy named Joe Cooper. I hear he's loaded up with all the latest detective techniques. And I hear he's tough as nails."

Zengo took this in. He liked the idea of not being the new guy any longer. But he wished the new detective were coming straight from the academy. Zengo was determined to finally shake the "rookie" moniker once and for all. "Let's see what I can find out about him," said Zengo, pulling out his phone. He opened the web browser and began to tap in the name of their soon-to-be colleague.

"Not now!" barked O'Malley. "Put down your phone for once. Rule number one, kid . . ."

Zengo rolled his eyes and sighed.

". . . keep your bill on the ball," said O'Malley.

"Right, right," said Zengo as he slipped his phone back into his pocket. But not before he glanced at the news alerts that popped up on the screen.

"Pandini sure is taking a beating in the polls," he said. "McGovern is ahead by more than twenty points."

"I thought I asked you to put that darn phone away," O'Malley barked.

"Rule number one, old-timer. Crime happens only in places where we're not paying attention."

"Hmpph." Zengo knew O'Malley didn't like it when he mouthed off. But he knew he had made a point, even if O'Malley didn't care to admit it.

Zengo observed a pack of teenagers with backpacks shuffling down the sidewalk. "O'Malley, look! Either this is a meeting of the Homework Club, or those are the punks we're looking for."

O'Malley trained his binoculars on the teenagers. "Yup, those backpacks are stolen. Knuckleheads didn't even bother removing the security tags." O'Malley's eyes tracked the suspects as they walked up a well-maintained pathway to one of the larger houses in the neighborhood.

"Think those boys are interested in a pizza?" asked Zengo.

"Roger that," said O'Malley.

The detectives had a guaranteed trick for getting teenage suspects to open the door. Zengo threw on a

Dominick's Delivery hat and reached for the pizza box in the backseat.

That's when the car radio crackled to life.

"Car one fifty-three . . ." Zengo and O'Malley leaned in and waited. Dispatches from Peggy back at the station always took a while. "Request . . . for your presence at . . . Pandini Towers."

Zengo wondered what was going down at Pandini Towers. That fancy fundraiser had enough security guards to form its own police squad. He grabbed the receiver. "But Peggy, we're about to close in on this shoplifting case!" They needed this collar to beat their fellow detectives Diaz and Lucinni in the monthly arrest competition. The winners won bragging rights and a free lunch.

"Sergeant Plazinski is . . . adamant that you . . . drop whatever you are doing . . . and get over there."

"Buckle up, kid," commanded O'Malley as he put the car into drive.

"But . . ." Zengo began as he motioned to the house where he was sure the teen perps were stashing their loot.

O'Malley swiped the receiver from Zengo and glared at him. "Ten-four, we're on our way."

Zengo sat back in his seat. He felt like a kid who had saved up all his tickets at the arcade and, just when he was about to cash them in for the big prize, his dad told him it was time to go. "What's another five minutes going to matter?"

"You don't question the sergeant, kid," said O'Malley. He pressed the button on the receiver. "What's the situation, dispatch? Over."

"There has been an attack on . . . Frank Pandini Jr. . . . in the middle of his . . . fundraiser."

O'Malley and Zengo slowly looked at each other.

They were both flabbergasted.

PANDINI TOWERS, 9:45 P.M.

When Zengo and O'Malley screeched to a halt at Pandini Towers a few minutes later, the chaos inside had already spread to the street. Satellite trucks from all seven Kalamazoo City television news teams jammed the driveway in front of the building. Reporters, their camera operators trailing them, were shoving microphones into the faces of the surging, screaming onlookers, trying to capture the panic of the moment for the benefit of viewers across the city—and, with any luck, nationwide. An assault on the leading candidate for mayor in a major city was big news indeed.

Zengo and O'Malley had to push their way through the crush of reporters to get close to a few beleaguered members of Pandini's security detail, who seemed to be trying to clear an open path from the main door of the building to an ambulance waiting at the curb. As they moved through, a brash young reporter shoved a microphone in O'Malley's face.

"Detective!" said the reporter. "Does the Platypus Police Squad have any official comment on the attack on Frank Pandini Jr.?"

O'Malley calmly said "no comment" and kept moving, but Zengo slowed down and eyed the microphone the reporter had extended over the police barricade. He flashed his biggest smile. "First of all, let me assure you that if anyone is trying to bring down Pandini's campaign, the Platypus Police Squad will get to the bottom of it."

O'Malley impatiently motioned to Zengo to follow him, but the reporter wasn't finished.

"Do you have any leads at this time?"

Cameras flashed. From behind Zengo, he could hear O'Malley hiss something, but it was drowned out in the din of people and traffic.

"Well, it's no secret Frank Pandini has his share of

enemies. We don't have any hard evidence yet, but if you ask me, I think—"

Before he could say more, he was grabbed roughly by the arm and tugged away. O'Malley's bill was right up in Zengo's face. "What the heck do you think you're doing, rookie?"

"Answering a few questions—what did it look like?"

"This isn't some shoplifting case we're dealing with here," O'Malley said. "Look around. These reporters are hungry for any scrap of news that they can turn into a national story. With a case this big, they don't care about the truth, they only care about what people will read and watch. It's *our* job to care about the truth, and so we can't go off speculating when we don't even have any facts." His expression softened. "Until we have something to report, we don't say a *word* to a reporter. You need to wise up if you're going to work a case like this, kid, you get me?"

Zengo was speechless. He'd rarely seen O'Malley this angry. Or this scared. And O'Malley had a point—they hadn't even examined the crime scene yet. Still, Zengo wasn't some kid fresh out of the academy anymore. Hadn't he been the one who exposed KC's illegal fish ring? And the corruption at the Disaster Dome?

He pulled his arm out of O'Malley's grip. "I got you." He made a big show of extending his flipper toward the tower lobby. "Why don't you lead the way, Detective? I doubt I'd be able to find the front door without following your lead."

O'Malley ignored his sarcasm and turned toward the tower entrance, but before he could take a step, the door burst open. A stretcher carrying Pandini

rolled out. At the sight of him, the crowd gasped.

Pandini, clearly in pain, one arm clutched to his side, nonetheless raised himself up enough to acknowledge the people assembled. "My fellow Kalamazooans!" he called, in a voice that lacked only a small bit of its usual power. "There's nothing to be worried about. It's going to take more than a thug with a boomerang to stop me!"

The crowd cheered. Zengo rolled his eyes. Pandini was already using this attack to his advantage.

As Pandini was rolled past Zengo and O'Malley, he signaled for his guard to stop. "I am glad two of KC's finest are already on the scene," he said to them. "If you ask me, this is a lot of fuss over nothing."

"I wouldn't say that, Mr. Pandini," said O'Malley. "An attack like this would be serious business even if

it hadn't been made on a person like yourself."

"Spoken like a future police commissioner," said Pandini. "I'm certainly happy to see you here too, Detective Zengo." He leaned in close to them. "For a second, I was afraid Plazinski was going to send those clowns Diaz and Lucinni."

Zengo laughed. He couldn't help himself. *At least Pandini knows talent when he sees it*, he thought.

O'Malley smiled as well. "You should get going, Mr. Pandini, but we'd like to talk to some of your guests and staff."

"Certainly. I've already instructed my campaign manager, Irving Myers, to make sure you have access to anything you need. And Detectives"—he looked right at Zengo—"I'd be most grateful if you could wrap this case up with your usual speed and efficiency. I said a few words to the crowd a moment ago because they need to know that I will not be bullied out of this race. But the truth is that this is nothing more than a distraction, and I want it dealt with so that this campaign can get back to talking about things that actually matter to the citizens of Kalamazoo City. They deserve no less."

For the second time outside Pandini Towers that night, Zengo was speechless. This was certainly a side of Pandini he'd never seen before. "We'll do our best, sir," he said.

Pandini nodded, then signaled to his handler and was whisked into the ambulance. Zengo watched until it turned a corner and disappeared.

"Hard guy to read," O'Malley said from beside him. "Can never tell if he's being honest, or just telling us what we want to hear."

"Either way," said Zengo, still thinking about Pandini's words, "we've got to solve this case."

POLICE LINE

PANDINI TOWERS PENTHOUSE, 10:00 P.M.

The elevator doors slid open at the penthouse, revealing a shaken and stirred crowd, equal parts offended and outraged that they were not permitted to leave. Beside the elevator doors was Bobby, the head of Pandini's security detail, still struggling to contain the guests.

"Thanks for holding all the potential witnesses," said O'Malley, nodding his approval. "Backup will be here in a couple of minutes."

"Some of your boys already are," said Bobby, pointing across the room to where a few members of the Platypus Police Squad were examining the area around the podium, as well as the large broken window directly behind it.

"Please tell me we can let these folks go home." Someone was approaching them. His name tag said "Irving Myers." *Pandini's campaign chief*, thought Zengo. Myers looked like he had just eaten a bucket of lemons.

Zengo put a comforting hand on Myers's shoulder. "Police work takes time. Our officers need to make sure that no stone is left unturned."

Myers deflated. Zengo almost felt sorry for him. Unhappy guests didn't make donations, and disappointing Frank Pandini Jr. must have awful consequences. Pandini's waitstaff was trying to cheer everyone up with free snacks and root beer, but that didn't seem to be doing much.

Zengo looked at the sea of angry faces. He had never seen so many powerful people in one place. Or so much bling. Every lady there was wearing as much jewelry as his mother probably had in her whole jewelry box. The scent of power in the room was very strong. Unless that was just the scent of strong perfume and cologne that Zengo was catching a whiff of.

Each person in that room could probably buy and sell the city several times over. Clearly they were not used to being told what to do.

Even though he was wearing his sweet leather jacket, Zengo still felt as if the crowd looked straight through him, as though he didn't exist. O'Malley was always talking about the divide in the city between the Rich and the Rest. That kind of thing never interested Zengo. But tonight was different. Here, in the most exclusive room of the city, surrounded by its most privileged citizens, he could see what that difference really meant.

One of the beat cops forced his way through the throng of tuxedos and dresses, and O'Malley gave him a nod.

"Casella, what gives?"

"Looks like we've got some sort of protester on our hands." Casella pointed to the banner.

Zengo read it aloud. "'Quit or else!' Hmph. Pretty direct, huh? We have any ID on the assailant?"

Casella shook his head. "His identity, his motive, and his current whereabouts are all a total mystery. Guy threw his boomerang, grazing Mr. Pandini and smashing the window, and just disappeared, right out the hole he'd made. We searched the streets below and nobody has been found. We're guessing whoever we're looking for, he can fly, but multiple guests confirmed we aren't dealing with any bird."

Zengo realized Irving Myers was hovering around them like a shadow, hanging on their every word. Normally, Zengo would have wanted their conversation to be private, but Myers was as close to Pandini's inner circle as anyone. Maybe he could lead them to some valuable information.

"We saw Pandini on his way to the ambulance," said O'Malley. "He didn't seem hurt too badly."

Casella shrugged. "Got his shoulder clipped. I've seen worse."

"We've all seen worse, Casella," said Zengo. "But nobody's ever taken a hit out on a mayoral candidate. We need to be on top of this. An assault on a mayoral candidate is an assault on the city itself."

"What are you, Pandini's newest PR rep?" Casella asked. "We're all doing our jobs here, rookie. O'Malley, I don't have time for lectures from your pet here. You want to take statements from some of these guests or what?"

Zengo opened his bill, but O'Malley put a hand on

his shoulder. "Look, kid," he whispered. "Why don't you go check out the window. Talking to some of these rich types can take some finesse. I'll meet you over there in a few minutes."

The young detective glared at them both. *I'm just trying to do my job too*, he thought, *if you guys would let me.* But he didn't say anything, just stormed off toward where Pandini had been delivering his speech.

The entire area surrounding the podium was blocked off with bright yellow caution tape. Zengo examined the scene, but the only thing out of the ordinary was the broken window, with its gaping hole open to the night sky. The wind blew hard this high up, and it whistled through the crack in the glass. Zengo snapped on a pair of rubber gloves and stepped over the barrier to take a closer look.

"These people didn't see much," said O'Malley, coming up behind him. Casella was with him too. "And even if they did, I think they're all a little too annoyed to tell us."

"Maybe you should have used a bit more of that finesse you were talking about," said Zengo. He leaned over and took a piece of broken glass in his flipper. "I don't think our assailant was trying to hit Pandini."

O'Malley ducked awkwardly under the caution tape. "Go on," he said. Zengo's partner actually seemed interested in his theory. *For once*, Zengo thought.

"Look at the angle at which the glass was broken. The boomerang was traveling to the right and grazed Pandini's left shoulder. If he was trying to hit him, he would have thrown on Pandini's right side so that, if he missed, the boomerang would hit him on the return trip. Who do you think this guy was?"

Myers stepped up to the caution tape, but stopped short of crossing it when all three cops barked at him to not take another step closer. "We don't know his name," Myers said. "But I can tell you he had a tail, and was wearing a mask."

"Pandini runs a tight ship," said Zengo. "His security

team is the best that money can buy. Whoever made it into this room armed with a concealed boomerang must have had help."

"Multiple witnesses told us that he was wearing the same uniform as the waitstaff," said Casella. "He was here the entire night, washing the dishes in the kitchen. But we took a statement from the company manager and the head chef, and neither of them remembers hiring him."

"The catering company is on Pandini's payroll," said O'Malley, stuffing his bill with a few more mini hot dogs that he nabbed from a passing waiter. "I'd recognize this distinct flavor anywhere. Frank's Franks."

"Well, I guess we won't need to dust the mustard for fingerprints," Zengo said. "Pandini claims to personally evaluate everyone who works for one of his companies. But if what you're saying is true, this guy wasn't actually an employee. And considering how many companies Pandini owns, criminals are bound to slip through the cracks."

"Or hop," said O'Malley through a mouthful of food, referring to the perpetrator of an illegal fish ring the Platypus Police Squad had taken down months ago.

"Let's look around the kitchen," said Zengo.

“Best idea you’ve had yet, kid,” said O’Malley, wiping the corners of his bill. “Casella, once all the guests are on record, tell ’em they’re free to go. But the waitstaff—I don’t want them going anywhere.”

Irving Myers led Detectives Zengo and O’Malley to the kitchen. It was a flurry of activity at the center of the penthouse. Everything was stainless steel and spotless—the kind of kitchen you see only on television shows. All except for the industrial-size sink, where dirty dishes teetered in a stack. Casella said, “We put all dishwashing on hold until we finish gathering evidence.”

“Besides,” said Zengo, “the only dishwasher on the

job just attacked Pandini and then flew out of the window of a skyscraper."

Irving Myers let out another sigh. "Couldn't we do this all tomorrow?" he asked. "It's been a long day."

"I'm afraid not," said Zengo. "The longer we wait, the colder the trail."

"We'd like to ask the head chef a few questions," said O'Malley.

"Naturally," said Myers, waving to a tall figure across the room. "Jacques? Please come over here."

Jacques clopped over to the detectives. He wore a pristine white chef's uniform, not a button askew—a remarkable feat considering how hectic this night must have been for him.

"You're the head chef at Black and White, aren't you?" asked O'Malley.

"I am, indeed," said Jacques. "Have been since Pandini opened the restaurant."

"Well, congratulations," said O'Malley. "Your joint is Kalamazoo's only three-star restaurant, is that right?"

Jacques nodded modestly.

"The suspect was disguised as one of your employees, is that right?" O'Malley continued.

"Yes, yes. Unfortunately, this is true," Jacques said

sheepishly. “He wore one of our white jackets, and had been washing dishes all night. But I’d never seen him before.”

“And you didn’t think to ask who he was, or what he was doing in your kitchen?” asked O’Malley.

“No, Detective, I didn’t. With this event coming up and things at Black and White continuing to heat up, we’d taken on a lot of new staff in recent weeks. I couldn’t keep track of everyone we’d hired.”

“So, you think he must have . . . what? Snuck in with the catering trucks?” asked Zengo.

Jacques locked eyes with Myers. “That would be my guess, yes—”

"Excuse me, Detectives," Myers interrupted, "it's after ten p.m., and the waitstaff is growing restless. I'm afraid I must insist that they be allowed to go home."

O'Malley turned to Officer Casella. "Ask the staff if any of them spoke to the suspect, if they picked up anything that might be able to tell us who he is or where we could find him. After that, they're free to go."

"You've got it." Casella nodded and then gathered the other uniformed cops to wrap up the evening's work.

"Mr. Myers, I see that the penthouse is equipped with security cameras," said O'Malley, pointing at the small lenses that dotted the ceiling. "We'd like the footage from tonight's event sent over to PPS headquarters before you leave tonight."

"Certainly," said the campaign manager.

"Thank you. Now, I imagine you want to go get a good night's rest. Tomorrow is going to be a busy day."

"It sure will be, Detective," he said. "Thank you for your assistance."

On the way out of the penthouse, Zengo stopped and gazed out the wall of windows at the skyline of Kalamazoo City. No wonder Pandini walked around town like he owned the place. From up here, he must feel like the king of the world.

"Heck of a view," said Zengo.

"It sure is," said O'Malley, who was staring at a waiter carrying the last plate of Frank's Franks.

PLATYPUS POLICE SQUAD HEADQUARTERS, 8:55 A.M.

It wasn't even nine a.m. yet, and Zengo was already on his second cup of hot chocolate. O'Malley was pouring his fourth cup of coffee.

Though they hadn't slept over at the station the night before, they might as well have. Reporters, hungry for a comment, had followed Zengo and O'Malley back to headquarters after they had left Pandini Towers, and the detectives mulled over the evidence until after two in the morning, when the reporters gave up and it was safe to go outside. The few hours they slept in their own beds had not been nearly enough. At dawn they were wading back through the sea of reporters again to enter the station, and were now at the evidence board, trying to make sense of last night's events.

One thing had been established: they had no lead on figuring out who the mysterious assailant was. The only thing they knew—he was a flying squirrel.

Zengo tapped at his wireless keyboard. Video footage of last evening's fundraiser flashed up on the flat-screen monitor. "We don't know this guy's name. None of the catering crew has any clue who he is. We don't even have a clear shot of his face. Pandini's team had only one security camera installed in the kitchen, and it was locked on the grill."

"Makes sense. I'm sure Pandini was more worried about the quality of the food than the possibility of a criminal posing as a dishwasher," commented O'Malley.

"By the time the assailant stepped out of the kitchen in view of the penthouse cameras, he already had his ski mask on." Zengo paused the video. "This blurry shot from the kitchen camera"—Zengo moved the footage forward three minutes—"and this one are the only images we have of his face before he put it on. And there's no question that mustache he's got is a fake."

O'Malley sipped his coffee. "What are we supposed to do? Drag every flying squirrel in the city into the station and hope one of them fesses up to the crime?"

"I've already made a list of every costume shop in town that sells squirrel mustaches," an unfamiliar voice called out from the back of the room.

Zengo and O'Malley swiveled in their seats to find a woman in a sharp pantsuit. Her arms were crossed. She leaned against the wall as if she'd been standing there for a while.

She walked to the evidence board. "Did you send screenshots of these two images to the forensic artists to create a composite of our guy here?"

Our guy? thought Zengo. *Who does this person think she is?*

That's when Zengo caught a glimpse of the badge pinned to her pocket.

"Darn those reporters!" Sergeant Plazinski burst through the door of the video bay and stopped short when he saw the stranger in the room. "Ah, gentlemen, I see that you've met the newest member of our team. Special Investigator Jo Cooper, I want you to meet Detectives Rick Zengo and Corey O'Malley. Two of our finest."

"Of course," said Cooper. "The detectives who cracked the KC Dome case. Nice work, boys."

"That's right." Plazinski clapped a flipper on her shoulder. "Cooper here is a real superstar. She's cut her teeth working for the state, but I persuaded her to bring her specialized training and expertise to KC. And just in time—we'll need her help with the recent developments."

Zengo watched O'Malley mouth the word "Jo." He could almost hear the gears turning in his partner's head.

"Nice to meet you," said Zengo.

"Welcome to the squad," added O'Malley.

"Thanks," Cooper said, not taking her eyes off the evidence board.

"Cooper's last assignment was Atlantis City," said Plazinski. "A second-rate police department has no

business employing a first-rate special investigator like Cooper. I've been trying to get her to come work with us for a while now."

"The casinos run Atlantis City from top to bottom," Cooper said. "I'm happy to be back in a city that's still got some semblance of honor and justice."

"Cooper is Kalamazoo born and raised," said the sergeant. "Quite the star of the field hockey team, if I remember."

"The *state champion* field hockey team." Cooper

smiled. Zengo remembered a field hockey team bringing a championship banner back to KC. He was in junior high then. If Cooper was older than he was, it wasn't by much.

"Sarge," O'Malley began, "do you really think this is the kind of case to break in a new cop? I've got my hands full with Zengo already."

Zengo's mouth fell open. "Thanks a lot, *partner*."

"I didn't mean it like that—" O'Malley began, but Plazinski cut him off.

"A candidate for mayor has been assaulted," said the sergeant. "Frank Pandini Jr., no less. This is the highest-profile case we've seen in years, and the media is already going crazy out there. We need to wrap this up quick and clean. I think Cooper can help us out with that. And I don't want to hear any more bill about it."

"Whenever you fellas are done," said Cooper, taking her flipper out of her pocket and examining it, "maybe you could send those shots to forensics."

"Was just about to," said O'Malley curtly.

"Good," said Cooper with a hard look. "While we wait for the image to come back, let's divide up this list of costume shops in town—"

"One more thing before you do," interrupted Plazinski. "I need to see all of you in my office. Diaz! Lucinni!" he barked suddenly. "I know you heard that!"

"Yes, sir," they said in unison. The two detectives slinked out from behind the door, where they'd been eavesdropping. *Clowns indeed*, thought Zengo.

SERGEANT PLAZINSKI'S OFFICE, 9:35 A.M.

"I don't have to tell you all how important this case is," said Sergeant Plazinski, pacing back and forth. He stopped in front of a photo of himself posing with Lieutenant Dailey, Zengo's grandfather. "It's been a long time since we've seen a case that has so shaken this city to its bones. And I need my best detectives working on it."

Zengo and O'Malley had taken the call last night to investigate the crime scene, which usually meant the case would be theirs, but Zengo had feared it wouldn't be that simple this time around. Diaz and Lucinni were looking at everyone sideways, and Jo Cooper had her eyes locked on Plazinski. Zengo balled his flippers into fists. This was just the sort of case he needed to finally prove himself. And he knew he was ready.

"I want the perp in custody YESTERDAY!" thundered Plazinski. He pulled up the window blinds and pointed at the sea of reporters still out on the precinct's front lawn. "I don't have to tell you all that the media is going to skewer us if we don't bring swift justice. Whoever the next mayor is, I don't want his first act to be shutting down the Platypus Police Squad."

"You got that right, Chief," said O'Malley, nodding. All the other detectives nodded too.

But who was going to get the case? The suspense was killing Zengo. The detectives snuck more glances at each other, then at Plazinski, who was looking down at his desk. The tapping of his pencil on the case file was the only sound in the room.

Finally, the chief looked up. "The lead detectives on this are going to be O'Malley . . ."

Zengo stood up and shot Diaz and Lucinni a look. *In your face*, he thought.

". . . and Jo Cooper."

Zengo froze. "What?" he squawked, saying it out

loud even though he hadn't meant to.

Jo Cooper, who had been standing a little apart from the others throughout the meeting, uncrossed her arms. "Roger that, sir." She turned to O'Malley and stuck out her hand. "Detective Corey O'Malley, it will be a pleasure to work alongside you," she said. "I've been hearing stories about you since before I entered the academy."

If O'Malley was upset about being assigned a new partner for this case, he wasn't showing it. In fact, he didn't say anything at all. He took Cooper's offered hand and gave her a polite smile.

Zengo's heart sank. O'Malley was supposed to be *his* partner, and this was supposed to be *his* case. A vision of Jo Cooper's smiling face right next to O'Malley's on the front page of the *Kalamazoo City Krier* swam before his eyes. How would he explain that to his parents?

"Now, Zengo," Plazinski continued, "wipe that scowl off your bill. You're not working this case with O'Malley because I've got another assignment for you. I got a call early this morning from Mr. Pandini himself. He's apparently pretty shaken up by this whole affair, and while he has more security on his payroll than the president, he's asking for some additional help. Namely, he's requested a member of the Platypus Police Squad to run lead on his protection detail for the rest of the campaign."

Zengo's bill flapped open. But before he could respond, O'Malley stepped forward.

"Wait a second here," he said. "You're not seriously considering sending the kid here to lead Pandini's protection team, are you?"

"That's exactly what I'm considering, O'Malley. Pandini requested Detective Zengo personally. He has been very impressed by Rick's work."

“But, but, there’s no way he’s ready to—” O’Malley sputtered.

“Look, Corey, it’s not up to you,” Plazinski interrupted. “And frankly, it’s not up to me either. I informed Mr. Pandini that this request was highly unusual, and that I’d agree to it only if Zengo said that he’d be willing—”

“I’ll do it,” Zengo broke in.

All eyes in the room turned to him.

"I'll do it," he repeated.

"But, rookie . . ." O'Malley took a step toward him and seemed to be searching for the right words. Zengo's gaze hardened. What was O'Malley's problem? Zengo wanted to keep working with O'Malley, of course, but this was a huge opportunity for him. Plus, being this close to Pandini could be just what was needed to find out who was responsible for the attack. He'd be right there in the middle of the action. Who knows what secrets he would uncover? Maybe he'd end up cracking the case himself!

"We don't know how many people are involved in this conspiracy to force Pandini out of the race," O'Malley finally said. "And we don't know what else they're willing to do to accomplish it. It could be dangerous. Heck, Pandini himself could be dangerous. We all know what happened the last time a Pandini ran this city—"

Plazinski slammed his palm down hard. "O'Malley, I have heard enough out of you," he said. "First off, Frank Pandini Jr. is not his father. And second, stop calling Detective Zengo a rookie. He has more than proven himself by this point. In fact, I think he might be the best detective Pandini could have asked for. None of us knows where this thug might strike next. Protecting Pandini could take some quick action—and, let's be honest here, you're not as fast on your flippers as you used to be. One more word out of you and you'll earn yourself an unplanned vacation, you get me?"

O'Malley looked down. "Yes, sir," he said.

Zengo opened his bill to say something to his partner, but as Jo Cooper slid up next to O'Malley and crossed her arms, he closed it. O'Malley wasn't his responsibility—Pandini was. And the sarge was right. If Zengo could nail this assignment all by himself, O'Malley definitely wouldn't be calling him "kid" or "rookie" anymore. O'Malley's protests played over and over in his head. *You're not seriously considering . . . It could be dangerous. . . .* Zengo's eyes burned and he had to look away. He stood up a little taller and adjusted his leather jacket. *I'll show O'Malley how a real detective does things*, he thought. *I'll show all of them.*

"Now, if there isn't anything else," said Plazinski, giving each of them a look that could cut glass, "get to work. Diaz, Lucinni—I want you running support for Cooper and O'Malley. Their wish is your command, got it? Let's start by taking a look at the venues for Pandini's upcoming campaign speeches. As for you, Zengo, Mr.

Pandini is expecting you at Bamboo." Plazinski leaned hard on his desk. "Remember, Detectives, we are all a team. Ain't no one else going to do this job for us, and those reporters out there ain't going to give us an inch of slack. It's up to us to solve this case and restore faith in this great city of ours."

A team, sure, thought Zengo. But to him, headquarters was starting to feel just a little bit crowded.

PLATYPUS
POLICE
SQUAD
TO SERVE AND PROTECT

PPS SQUAD ROOM, 9:45 A.M.

The detectives were absorbed back into the hustle and chaos of the precinct. Phones rang, blue-uniformed officers led shackled criminals to and from their holding cells, and Peggy struggled to hold back a couple of reporters who must have tried to sneak into the squad room.

Zengo gathered his things and shut down his computer. He looked up to see his partner standing over him with an apologetic smile on his face. Zengo did not smile back.

"What do you want, O'Malley?" he said. Zengo

didn't have anything to say to him, and he could sense a classic O'Malley lecture coming on.

"Listen, kid—" O'Malley caught himself and fidgeted with his tie. "I mean, Rick. I'm sorry about what I said in there. You're a great detective—you've saved my tail more times than I can count. But like I said last night, this isn't your average case. There are going to be eyes on you all the time. And I'm not just talking about the reporters."

"And maybe you'd rather those eyes were on you?" Zengo wheeled on his partner. "Is that it? Are you jealous I got chosen for this assignment? The *rookie* got selected over the great Corey O'Malley?"

"No, that isn't what I'm saying." O'Malley put his hands on his hips. "Now you *are* acting like a little kid."

"Just because you can't admit that you're upset Pandini picked me and not you—"

"I didn't come over here to argue about this, Rick. Believe whatever you want to believe. But I'm just looking out for you. Take my advice: watch your back with Pandini. It seems to me he's willing to do whatever it takes to win this election. It's all he cares about."

Zengo blinked. Wasn't O'Malley the one who was

always telling Zengo not to jump to conclusions about Pandini?

"I'm just telling you to be careful, is all," O'Malley finished.

"I can handle myself," said Zengo. "Plazinski thinks so. It's high time you did as well."

"Fair enough." He dropped his tie and stepped back. "In that case, here's the deal. You're going to be at a lot of rallies, a lot of inner-circle events. You'll be with Pandini every time he's out in public. We'll need you to keep an eye on every person who seems even a tiny bit suspicious."

"I'm a detective, O'Malley," said Zengo, grabbing the last couple of files he needed from his drawer. "That's what I do. Rule number one: pay close attention to the world around you. Remember?"

He tucked his badge into his inner pocket. O'Malley opened his bill to say more but then closed it as Cooper approached with a mile-high stack of papers.

"I've run a background check on Pandini's campaign manager, Irving Myers," she said in her brisk, businesslike voice. "I think we should start our search by investigating the election team, to see if anyone isn't who they say they are. This guy Irving, he's run some very successful campaigns, but no one wins in this game without breaking a few rules. He may have a hidden agenda. And that might be the case for others on the team as well. We need to know everything we can before we go sniffing around his business."

She handed O'Malley half the stack. *Maybe O'Malley finally got the partner he always wanted,* thought Zengo.

Looks like Cooper is even more methodical than he is.

Zengo threw on his sunglasses and walked out of headquarters without looking back.

BAMBOO, 10:25 A.M.

Zengo brought his car to a stop in Bamboo's empty parking lot. Pandini's popular club didn't open for lunch for another hour. He walked across the pavement, pushed open the club's doors, and was greeted with a handshake by Pandini's bodyguard, Bobby. It was quite the contrast to Zengo's first visit to Bamboo. Bobby had almost thrown him out before he'd even been in here a minute. Things were a lot different than they were back on his first case. *He* was a lot different. He removed his sunglasses.

"Thank you for coming, Detective, we've been

expecting you," Bobby said. He motioned over to the bar, where the bartender was changing out the root beer kegs and testing the taps. "Carpy, please show Detective Zengo some hospitality with one of our award-winning root beer floats."

"No need," said Zengo. "You'll have plenty of paying customers to serve soon."

"Nonsense," chuckled the koala, who barely reached the bar top. "You're part of the family now. Families take care of one another." He plopped a scoop of vanilla into a freshly poured root beer and slid it down the bar, where Bobby caught it and handed it to the detective.

Zengo didn't like being called "family" by these characters, but man, that bubbling vanilla smelled delicious. Plus, it would be rude to turn down such a generous gesture.

"Thank you," said Zengo as he took a big foamy sip. Bobby raised an eyebrow and handed him a napkin. "Oh, right," said Zengo, a little embarrassed as he wiped his bill.

"Come on. Mr. Pandini is waiting for you."

Bobby led Zengo to a panel in the wall that opened, revealing a dark stairway that wound its way upward.

Zengo had never noticed this door before. He followed Bobby up to Pandini's second-floor office.

It was an impressive space. Frank Pandini Jr. spared no expense. One entire wall was a huge one-way window—it looked just like a wall from down in the club, but from up here someone could watch everything happening on the floor. There were video screens and computers all around the room, lots of comfy couches, and even his own root beer bar. He could probably run his entire empire from this room—and in style, too.

The candidate sat behind a huge mahogany desk. He was deep in discussion with Irving Myers, who sat on one of the sleek chairs across from him. "Ah, Detective Zengo," he said, glancing up. "I'll be with you in just a moment."

Pandini's walls were adorned with photos of the mogul with Kalamazoo City's most famous and upstanding citizens. Each black-and-white photo was crisply matted and framed. It looked like an art gallery. This was a collection of all the most powerful people in town. There was even a photo of Pandini with his opponent in the mayoral race, Patrick McGovern, presumably taken during less competitive times.

"Your poll numbers have transformed overnight," said Myers, indicating a row of numbers on a chart he was showing Pandini. "In an instant poll taken by Channel Five Action News following the incident, your favorables shot up to eighty-eight percent. This is exactly the shot in the arm the campaign needed!"

Pandini exhaled heavily and lifted his arm that sat in a sling.

"Apologies, Mr. Pandini," Myers backtracked. "Poor choice of words."

"I won't have us playing the victim in the press," Pandini said. "If we're going to win, we're going to do it on the back of the campaign platform that you and

I crafted—making this city the best it can be. I want you out there talking to reporters, turning their attention back to the issues that matter. I'll be out of this sling in a couple of days, and I don't want to be taking any more questions about the attack."

"Mr. Pandini, if I may." Myers adjusted his glasses. "This isn't my first rodeo. Opportunities like this don't come around very often, and—"

"You heard me, Irving. Three days to quash this story, and I don't want to hear another word about it. Hopefully by then the assailant will have been apprehended, and we can forget this entire thing ever happened. Speaking of which—it's lovely to see you, Detective Zengo." Pandini flashed his signature smile. "Mr. Myers, if you don't mind, I'd like to speak to my new head of security."

"Of course." Myers gathered up his papers. "Remember, we've got the rally tonight at Kalamazoo City University." He made his way to the stairs. Bobby followed him out, leaving Zengo and Pandini alone together.

Pandini gestured to the other seat in front of the desk, and Zengo sat down, careful not to spill his root beer float. The last thing he needed to do his first day

on the job was ruin one of Pandini's expensive chairs.

"Detective Zengo, I can't thank you enough for coming here, and for your willingness to help with my security detail."

"Please, Mr. Pandini," Zengo found himself saying, "call me Rick." If he was going to get close enough to Pandini to find out what was going on, the best way was to keep things friendly.

Pandini smiled. "All right, then. Rick, I'll be straight with you. My security guys are good, but I fear even they aren't prepared for what I think might be out there." Pandini lifted his left arm again. "Despite what

I just said to Mr. Myers, I fear this attacker wasn't working alone. I believe there is someone behind this, and that he or she will try again. I need someone who can not only protect me, but also help put an end to these attacks once and for all."

Zengo nodded. "I understand. But . . . why me?"

Pandini leaned in. "You love this city, Detective. I've known that from the moment I first met you, right down there next to the bar. And when you didn't hesitate to chase a criminal through the crowded dance floor below us, I knew you'd stop at nothing to make sure this city is safe. Now, I love this city as well, and I too have worked tirelessly to turn it into one of the most enviable and respected cities in the whole country. But you and I both know—we can do better. This city can be better. Better schools for our children. Better care for our elderly. Better resources for those in need. Safer streets at all hours of the day, in all parts of the city. That's why I am running for mayor—to make a difference. Not just for the rich, who—let's face it—are the ones who have most benefited from my many businesses. But for everyone, rich and poor alike."

Pandini stared hard at Zengo, and Zengo tried to

return his stare with equal intensity. It was not easy. Once again, Zengo was moved by what Pandini was saying. But was he being honest? Or was it just a very well-rehearsed campaign speech?

"I know what you see when you look at me," said Pandini. "And I can't say that I blame you."

Zengo didn't know what to say. "I'm not exactly sure what you mean. . . ."

"When you look at me, you think about your grandfather," Pandini continued. "My father brought much pain and grief to you and your family. Just as he did to this city."

Pandini paused and his eyes lost focus, looking off past Zengo, who was frozen to the spot. Pandini's father had committed many crimes as Kalamazoo City's most notorious crime boss, including killing Zengo's grandfather. The detective began to sweat, and gripped the leather arms of the chair tighter.

"My father brought shame to this city," Pandini said finally. "It's been my life's mission to reverse the damage that he did. And it's been an uphill battle. But nothing could prepare me for this campaign. In business, it doesn't matter what anyone thinks of you—all they care about is whether your restaurant is the best, or your gym, or your nightclub, or your ballpark. But running for mayor . . . this is different. What people think of you matters just as much as what you do. And no matter what I do, it's almost impossible to change what people think of me, of my name. None of them know the real me, they know only my image, my family, my past. It hasn't been easy, convincing them who I really am. That I'm ready for this. That I can lead this city. Can you understand that, Detective?"

Zengo certainly knew what it was like to be judged by someone in your family who came before you. He thought about his grandfather, and the hopes his parents had for the police lieutenant Zengo might become. And he thought about O'Malley, who kept calling him "rookie," even after everything Zengo had done, all the cases he'd solved, all the criminals who would still be on the street if it wasn't for him.

Zengo had never trusted Pandini. He'd never get over what Pandini's father had done. And he still wasn't sure that the selfless little speech Pandini had just given about making Kalamazoo a better place for every citizen, rich or poor, was genuine. But right now, Zengo couldn't help but feel like Pandini might be the only one who really knew how he felt.

Finally, Zengo said, "I can understand that, Mr. Pandini."

"If we're going to work together," said Pandini, smiling, "I must insist you call me Frank."

Despite everything, Zengo smiled too.

The office door swung open and Bobby entered with a plateful of fresh, steaming fish. He lumbered across the room and placed the tray before Zengo.

"Caught by Kalamazoo City's own fishermen," Pandini said proudly. "The best KC bass money can buy."

Pandini might care about the less fortunate, thought Zengo, *but he sure doesn't eat like them*. Was all that talk about the poor just baloney? Zengo supposed it didn't matter. He was at Pandini's side to protect him, not to fall for his campaign promises. And certainly not to indulge in all this extravagance.

Still . . . Zengo loved fresh bass. The smell of the fish just below his bill made his mouth water. *This assignment doesn't have to be* all *work*, Zengo thought. He picked up his fork and dug in.

PANDINI FOR MAYOR
VOTE PANDINI

KALAMAZOO CITY UNIVERSITY, STUDENT UNION, 6:00 P.M.

The Student Union was rocking when Pandini, flanked by Zengo and Bobby, arrived for the Youth Rally. Like the evening before, the area around the building was swarming with noisy reporters, climbing over one another like ants at a picnic, each trying to get as close as possible to the man of the hour. Zengo glanced at every face but saw no one who looked suspicious. He had his work cut out for him that evening—not only did he have to keep a sharp eye on all the students, but he also had to keep these motley newshounds on his radar.

Zengo noticed the "U" was a lot spiffier than just a few years before, when he had gone to school there. He also noticed an imposing bronze plaque with a portrait of Frank Pandini Jr. mounted in the lobby. Zengo figured the mogul had provided the funding to give the building its proud new look. *Not a surprise.*

"Quite a crowd," Pandini murmured as Bobby stepped in front, sticking out his elbows as widely as possible to clear the path ahead of them. "And by that I mean, quite a crowd *of reporters.*" Still, he smiled broadly as the flashbulbs popped around him.

Pandini Enterprises had just opened a new Frank's Franks stand on campus, and Irving Myers was already there, handing out fistfuls of coupons for free hot dogs to a crowd of students. He gave the rest of the coupons to a nearby student volunteer and strode up to the candidate. "Quite a turnout, eh?"

"Great work, Myers," said Pandini. "Especially summoning that welcoming committee." He nodded back at the scrum of reporters. If possible, Myers grinned even more broadly and bobbed his head up and down.

Gesturing at the starry-eyed students who surrounded them, Myers said loudly, "Would you like to greet some of the young citizens who have volunteered their time to put this event together?"

"I'd like nothing better!" said Pandini, just as loudly.

Bobby continued to sweep a path before them as the candidate and his manager moved through the crowd together, Pandini waving at the smiling onlookers with his good arm.

Zengo hung back, continuing to scan the crowd for anything out of the ordinary. Though it was unlikely that the perp would make another hit so soon after last evening's failed attempt, Zengo was still on the lookout for bushy tails. But all he saw were college students, none of them bright-eyed—some looked like they had just rolled out of bed, others looked like they had been up for way too long in the library.

There was one person there who was out of place. It was an older guy, leaning against a wall, trying to blend in. Corey O'Malley was sipping a cup of red

punch, his pockets crammed with Frank's Franks coupons. Of course, O'Malley was working his own case, but the sight of him made Zengo's fur rise, just a little. Pandini was *his* responsibility. He gave a short, civil nod to his former partner.

"How's it going, rook—I mean, Rick?" said O'Malley.

Zengo pretended not to notice the slipup. "Everything is under control," he said. "How about you? Anything turning up in the *archives*?" Zengo pronounced that last word sourly—like he had just drunk pickle juice.

"We've been combing through stacks of paperwork on Pandini's various business associates," said O'Malley. "The guy's made a lot of enemies in this city, but no one with any connection to the attack. Glad we did our research before wasting time running around Kalamazoo."

Zengo's eyes slid over to O'Malley, who held his gaze. Was that a dig, or just one of his typical bits of overbearing advice? Zengo decided to ignore it and, stiffening his shoulders, changed the subject. "So, where's Detective Cooper?" he asked. "Is she out asking the teachers for more homework?"

O'Malley nodded for Zengo to look behind him.

Cooper was standing about a foot away, one eyebrow raised. She had obviously overheard Zengo.

"H-h-hi . . ." he stumbled.

"Hello, Detective Zengo," said Cooper coolly.

O'Malley cleared his throat. "Say, Jo, I got us some extra coupons," he said, handing half of his stash to Cooper.

"Excellent," she said with a short nod, tucking them away in her jacket pocket.

Zengo couldn't believe this buttoned-down detective ate that crud too. At least she didn't spill mustard on her shirt like O'Malley did.

"Any new findings, Detective?" she asked. "I hope you realize we're counting on you to bring anything unusual to our attention."

Was she giving him orders? Zengo looked back and forth at Cooper and O'Malley. They stood shoulder to shoulder, their faces showing no expression. Zengo felt a pang of jealousy, but he kept it hidden.

"I'm all over this situation, Cooper," he said, with just a touch of edge in his voice. "But it's kind of hard to keep a lookout for suspicious squirrels with all those reporters in the way. It's a good thing you two decided to show up here. I could use a hand. See any bushy tails anywhere?"

"Don't tell me you think every squirrel is a potential perp?" said O'Malley.

"I'm not looking for any old squirrel," said Zengo. "I'm looking for *the* squirrel. Are you guys going to help me or not?"

Before the conversation got hotter, they were interrupted by a familiar voice coming from somewhere around their knees. All three detectives looked down.

"Well, well, well . . . looks like the Platypus Police Squad family is growing. . . ." Derek Dougherty could barely be seen behind his camera. It wasn't a gigantic camera, just a regular-size camera held skillfully by a small chameleon.

"Who's the pretty lady?"

Cooper crouched down, removed her sunglasses, and put her bill right in Derek's face, pushing his camera to the side. "My name is Detective Jo Cooper. It's a pleasure to meet you." She grasped Derek's hand and shook it so firmly that the reporter's bugged-out eyes bugged out even more.

Derek attempted to shake the pain out of his hand. "Well, glad to know that the Platypus Police Squad has its best people on the case."

"What are *you* doing over here, anyway?" said Zengo. "Shouldn't you be over there with all the other muckrakers?" He indicated the crowd of reporters shoving their way as near to the stage at the front of the room as possible

"Besides," said O'Malley, "I heard Patrick McGovern

is picking up some groceries across town. Isn't that a more typical story for the *Krier*'s front page?" The *Kalamazoo City Krier* was the city's biggest newspaper, and it had officially endorsed McGovern for mayor. It also seemed to go out of its way to make Pandini look bad whenever possible.

"Hardy-har," said Dougherty. "I cover any and all events around KC. And what could be more interesting than Detective Rick Zengo here providing security for old Pandini Jr.? It's such a fascinating story! I can't wait to snap some pictures of you with your new pal, Ricky."

Zengo was not amused. And he loathed being called "Ricky" by anyone who was not his mother.

Derek continued. "The Pandini family isn't exactly known for its ability to stay on the right side of the law. There's bound to be something shady going on in this campaign. Wouldn't you agree, Ricky?"

"That's Detective Zengo to you. And I'm not here to comment on Pandini's candidacy, just to protect the candidate himself." Zengo returned to scanning the crowd, an attempt to brush off the pushy questions. But Derek wasn't known for his subtlety.

"Yes, it really is the most curious of circumstances,

isn't it? Why again are you working as Pandini's hired arm?"

"Oops," said O'Malley, tipping his cup and sending a waterfall of red punch down on Derek Dougherty.

"HEY!" Derek shouted while stepping to the side and looking down on his now-pink shirt. "What are you thinking? I should—"

Derek's rant was interrupted by a tap-tapping noise emanating from the big speakers at the front of the room. The detectives and the journalist looked up to the podium, where an enthusiastic young volunteer was trying to get the attention of the audience. Behind her hung a banner that read "Students for Pandini."

Zengo needed to get to the front of the room, and fast. "Nice chatting with you all, but I'm on duty," he said, hustling away from the others. How was he going to make his way through the surging crowd? He drew himself up to his full height and hoped he seemed intimidating. "PLATYPUS POLICE SQUAD! COMING THROUGH!" he shouted, over and over. And to his surprise, students actually moved out of his way.

But reporters and photographers crowded the edge of the stage, and he couldn't get one of them to budge, no matter how hard he tried. He even pulled out his badge and waved it around, but no response. Finally he caught Bobby's eye, just behind the curtain at the edge of the stage. Bobby came forward and scowled his darkest scowl, and finally enough reporters moved aside that Zengo was able to climb up and join him.

He and Bobby stepped behind the curtain, where Pandini and Myers were discussing the speech he was set to deliver. Pandini was taking his sling off, and Myers was trying to stop him. "Optics, Frank, optics," said Myers, indicating the reporters and photographers. "We've got to keep up the sympathy play."

"Nonsense," said Pandini. "The people want to see a strong candidate, not a weak one."

At the podium, the student volunteer had finally gotten control of the crowd. "What an amazing turnout!" she said. "We are so proud to welcome the next mayor of Kalamazoo City!"

The crowd roared. She motioned for them to be quiet again. "He is here to talk to us about the issues that matter to us! So please give a big KCU welcome to Mr. Frank Pandini Jr.!"

Pandini took off his sling and handed it to Myers as he stepped through the curtain. "How can I help him if he won't listen to my advice?" Myers muttered.

The crowd erupted once more as Pandini stood before them. Students pumped their fists and held up posters provided by the Pandini campaign. It made for some fantastic photos, and camera flashes popped all throughout the room.

"Thank you, thank you!" said Pandini as he motioned for the crowd to settle down. "What a very warm welcome, thank you!" Pandini waited for the last hoot and holler to subside, and then took an additional beat for dramatic effect before going into his prepared remarks.

Zengo had never heard Pandini's stump speech before. He expected it to be a variation on his usual theme—"Your city—better!" But instead, Pandini was on a new tack.

"You students are the future," he began. "And as your mayor, I'm going to put your health and safety at the very top of my agenda."

The students cheered again. Zengo was interested to know where this was going.

"In all my years as a successful businessman, I am proud to say that I have created many, many opportunities for you all to lead better and healthier lives.

The Pandini sports facility here at the university for example."

He was interrupted once more by cheers.

"Thank you, thank you. And of course, my restaurants, even the cafeteria right here on campus, which I also operate, serve nothing but delicious, healthful food—"

One student shouted, "What about Frank's Franks?" *A heckler after my own heart*, thought Zengo.

But Pandini didn't miss a beat. "Yes, even Frank's Franks. As I stand here, Frank himself is working with my expert chefs to reformulate his hot dogs to be healthy and nutritious—"

The crowd moaned its disapproval.

"AND delicious!" said Pandini. "You won't taste the

difference—but you'll *feel* the difference! They will be your hot dogs—*better*!"

The crowd recovered and cheered again.

Pandini leaned forward and gripped the edges of the podium. Even from behind him, from offstage, Zengo could see Pandini was about to get to the heart of his message. And he was going to make sure that every eye in the room was on him.

"And that is why, today, here at Kalamazoo City

University, one of the finest universities in the world, I am proud to announce that from this day forward, for the protection of you, the future of our fair city, I will no longer be serving nut or nut-related products in any of my eating establishments!"

The crowd fell silent. Zengo was puzzled, and obviously they all were too. No nuts?

Pandini pulled some papers from his jacket pocket and waved them before the crowd. "I have been studying the rise of nut-related allergies in our city for years—one in three children born today is afflicted. How many of you fall into this category?"

Zengo was shocked when almost half the students, and even a few of the reporters, raised their hands. The crowd murmured.

Pandini continued. "And yet, virtually all this city's restaurants continue to serve food laden with nuts. It accounts for hundreds of emergency room visits every year. That's why I'm here today, to take a stand. And in my administration, not only will nuts be banned in my restaurants, they will be banned throughout Kalamazoo City!"

The clapping started softly but quickly grew into loud applause and cheers. Pandini had won them over.

Was this his new strategy? To appeal to the youngest voters? Zengo had to admit that it was refreshing to hear someone who took young people seriously, for once. He found himself feeling a little proud, for reasons he didn't quite understand.

That's when Zengo noticed something that sent his heart racing. At the far end of the room, just by the main entrance, a bushy tail bobbed up behind the faces of the students. Was it possible? Was the assailant about to strike again?

Zengo didn't hesitate for a moment. He jumped down from the stage and dashed across the hall, maneuvering once more through the dense crowd. Out of the corner of his eye, he saw that Detective Cooper was also on the run, headed in the same direction. Zengo sped up. No way he was letting the newbie nab this collar right from under his nose. That's when he felt a sharp tug on his own collar. Cooper was trying to stop him.

"What are you doing?" coughed Zengo. He pushed her webbed hands away and looked to see the back of a bushy tail as it neared the door of the Student Union. The squirrel was escaping.

Running hard, Zengo managed to catch up. He

grabbed the suspect by the shoulder and got right in his face. “Stop right there!”

“Sorry?” said the mild-mannered squirrel as he fixed his glasses. “I’m not certain I am following you. May I help you?”

Cooper, running at full speed, caught up with them. “Let him go, Zengo! He’s the dean of the university!”

“I, uh . . .” Zengo searched for the right words as

he took in the squirrel before him. For one, he wasn't even a flying squirrel. For two, he should have realized immediately that this guy was someone important, with his necktie and his little professorial glasses and his briefcase. He released his shoulder and looked down at his webbed feet.

Jo Cooper stepped up. "Dean Reynolds, how nice to see you again!"

"Ah, Ms. Cooper, how lovely! Is this a friend of yours here? What is the meaning of all this?"

"Just a little police work, sir. This here is one of Pandini's staffers. It's a real tough campaign, and they're just trying to get out the vote with the rally here."

Zengo opened his bill, but Cooper elbowed him in the ribs so hard he could barely breathe, let alone utter a word.

"Very well, then," said Dean Reynolds. "It's always exciting to see our students engaged with the political process. You'd do better to be a little less aggressive with your campaigning tactics, son." The university dean straightened out his jacket and turned to leave. "Now, if you'll excuse me, I must attend a trustees meeting."

“What was that about?” Cooper asked after Dean Reynolds had left, smacking Zengo on the side of his head.

“Why did you tell him I was a part of Pandini’s campaign? Do you really think—”

“Knucklehead! Do you want the university dean calling up Plazinski to chew out his squad? I just saved your tail!”

Suddenly, they heard screams coming from the Student Union. Cooper's radio crackled to life. It was O'Malley.

"Cooper! Cover the exits! Another attack was just made on Pandini! It was another flying squirrel!"

Cooper and Zengo immediately drew their boomerangs.

"I'll cover the front," said Zengo.

"Roger," said Cooper. She radioed back to O'Malley, "We're on it." She sped off toward the rear of the building.

The blood raced through Zengo's veins as he gripped the cold, metal boomerang and ran out the door. He held it aloft, ready to launch it at the sign of a threat. Zengo flinched at the sound of breaking glass above—someone had broken the skylight. He saw a shadowy figure emerge onto the roof and spread its gliders to dive off, bushy tail and all.

"Platypus Police Squad! Freeze!" Zengo shouted.

The flying squirrel didn't flinch. Zengo had no choice. He closed one eye and launched his boomerang at the squirrel. It sliced through the air like a razor and clipped the perpetrator's wing flap. But he took off anyway, gliding toward a nearby treetop.

PANDINI FOR MAYOR

Zengo caught the boomerang on its return and raced to the tree. But the squirrel had the advantage and was soon out of boomerang range, gliding from tree to tree, making a quick escape.

O'Malley and Cooper were soon by his side, O'Malley operating the walkie-talkie to summon Diaz and Lucinni to join the pursuit. He looked at Zengo. "What are you doing here?" he said. "Go check on Pandini!"

Of course he was right, but Zengo hated to admit it. He turned tail and ran back into the Student Union. The crowd was in a panic. Pandini had not been hit, evidently, but had fallen over onto his bad arm. And the pesky reporters were still shoving their way up to the front. Bobby was doing all he could to hold them back.

When Myers caught sight of Zengo he was furious.

"Where have you been?" he snapped. "You were supposed to PREVENT this from happening! What is WRONG with you?"

Zengo was too flustered and out of breath to reply, so he hung his head and tried to resume his position by Pandini's side. Pandini gave him a cold glance, then returned to the crowd. "There's nothing to worry about!" he shouted. "I'm okay!"

"PANDINI! PANDINI! PANDINI!" chanted the crowd.

"I'm a fighter," he said, climbing to his feet and standing at the podium once more. "And I will never stop fighting for you!"

He waved, and reporters swarmed up onto the stage. Pandini ignored them and walked past Zengo without a glance in his direction.

Zengo was ashamed. He would find a way to make this up to Pandini.

PLATYPUS POLICE SQUAD HEADQUARTERS, 7:45 P.M.

Back at his desk, weary after his long day but too unsettled to go home, Zengo opened his computer screen to the *Kalamazoo City Krier* online edition. As he expected, the lead story, beneath a three-inch-high headline, was CANDIDATE PANDINI ATTACKED AGAIN. Zengo did not recognize the byline—Melinda Smuthers. Probably one of the reporters he had to push past. There were shots of Pandini down, with Myers standing above him and Bobby holding everyone back.

Zengo skimmed the piece. The reporter complimented Pandini's bravery and panache, and praised his plans to limit nuts in his restaurants and, once elected, in all of Kalamazoo City. As averse as Pandini was to using these attacks to his advantage, it was clear that they were working—another article featured an instant poll that showed his support was continuing to rise. *Irving Myers must be pleased*, Zengo thought.

He scanned the other headlines and stopped short. Derek Dougherty had gotten his hooks in, all right. INEXPERIENCED DETECTIVE NOT READY FOR PRIME TIME. In his story, Dougherty took Zengo to task for failing to prevent Pandini from being attacked again. He shuddered, shut off his monitor, and turned away, hoping O'Malley, sitting just a few feet away, didn't pick up on what was going on. He was out of luck, though. He saw O'Malley was looking at the *Krier* on his computer as well.

"Tough break, Rick," said O'Malley.

Zengo blinked. This was the second time in one day that O'Malley had called him Rick. Still, he didn't want to let his old partner know that the pesky reporter had gotten under his fur. "It's okay," he said. "I guess I deserved it."

“This case is all anyone wants to talk about,” said O’Malley. “Figures a little creep like Dougherty would use the opportunity to take a lowball swipe like that.”

Zengo really wanted to change the subject. “What matters more is stopping these attacks.”

“You got that right,” said O’Malley.

Zengo had turned his monitor on again, now pulling up surveillance footage from the rally. There were a few screen captures of the assailant, but all were blurry.

"I don't think that we're dealing with a flying squirrel," Zengo said. It was a theory that he had been mulling over in his brain all evening, but he was now confident enough to say it out loud. "This whole thing just doesn't add up. I'm beginning to think we're looking at some sort of conspiracy here. I'm not certain this is even the same squirrel as last night."

"Well, that's a theory. Where are you getting that from?"

Zengo swiveled his computer screen and pointed. "Slightly different markings on the tail. Noticed it when I saw the perp earlier today."

O'Malley took a moment to absorb all of this. "Well, maybe. Don't forget about the fake mustache. We could be dealing with someone who is adept at disguise. The tail could be a dye job."

Zengo swiveled his screen back. "Maybe. Either way, those wing flaps were fakes. I'm positive that I clipped him with my boomerang, and he didn't even flinch."

O'Malley was silent, mulling over what Zengo had said.

"This won't happen again. I'm going to stick by Pandini at every public event until we solve this case.

And I'll be keeping an eagle eye out for every suspicious character who gets close to him—whether at headquarters or at his campaign events."

"That'll keep you busy," said O'Malley. "He does seem to attract shady characters—and in my opinion the shadiest of them all are right there on his own staff." He pointed at the *Krier* on his screen. "And all the positive press these attacks are generating . . . it just doesn't smell right to me. If the *true* purpose of this conspiracy you're talking about is to bring Pandini's campaign down, seems to me like it ain't working. Who's benefiting from this? Pandini, that's who."

"I'm really trying hard to keep an open mind," said Zengo, noticing O'Malley's expression change. "I mean, about Pandini's inner circle. So far nobody has done anything to get in my way. They've all welcomed me. And yeah, Irving Myers seems to want Pandini to take as much advantage of the publicity from these attacks as he can, but that's a long way from saying he'd ever do anything to harm Pandini."

"Yeah, but what about Bobby? And that creep Carpy? They're not exactly model citizens. And if Pandini becomes mayor, those are all the ones who stand to benefit the most, cushy jobs in the mayor's office and all. I'm just saying I'd suggest you watch your back—and your front—when you're with that crowd."

"I hear you," said Zengo. "In the meantime, I'm not going to jump to any more conclusions. I have to admit, Pandini's been straight with me since he brought me on. And it's hard to argue with his record. He's given a ton of money to the city."

"Not a day goes by when he doesn't mention it in some way," said O'Malley. "McGovern's done quite a bit for the city, too. He's spent his life fighting against corruption as district attorney. Plus, he's from my side of town—where folks work hard for every penny. McGovern has never forgotten his roots. And he thinks a mayor's job is to do good—for everyone. Can you say the same for Pandini? Sure, he's built buildings, stadiums even—but the only time I ever saw him standing up for reform was when he was clearing the path for his own run for mayor."

"You have an interesting point . . ." said Zengo, thinking. "Any chance McGovern might be behind these attacks?"

"Seems a little obvious to me," said O'Malley. "And

he was leading in the polls prior to the attack. Why take the risk?"

But Zengo wasn't sure, and he could tell O'Malley wasn't either. McGovern was Pandini's opponent, and he had a lot to gain from Pandini dropping out of the race. Maybe Mr. McGovern was worth a closer look.

ZENGO HOUSE, 6:50 A.M.

Patrick McGovern's campaign ads played during every single commercial break throughout *Kalamazoo City Today*, the city's morning news program, blaring as usual from the Zengo family's kitchen television. Each one featured the district attorney in front of local landmarks, like the library and the zoo, in middle-class neighborhoods like Corey O'Malley's. Every commercial highlighted his humble beginnings while taking digs at Pandini's past. Though this was just politics as usual, Zengo had begun to think it was not fair to smear someone because of what his father had done years ago. He pondered his suspicions about McGovern that he had voiced last night. Could he possibly be behind this conspiracy?

"We all know what my opponent's father did to this city," Patrick McGovern's voice intoned as old black-and-white photographs of crime scenes flashed across the screen. "There was the infamous Kalamazoo City Bank robbery, which nearly shuttered the doors of the historic KC institution. It took us decades to recover. Then, there was the Great Fishing Boat Attack." Another photograph appeared, this one of sullen fishermen, their arms crossed. One held a sign reading "No boats = no fish." It was rumored, but never proven, that when KC fishermen refused to pay a special fee to Pandini Sr., he had their vessels sunk and made a fortune by importing his own fish from the black market.

And then came the lowest blow of all—a photo of Zengo's late grandfather. "And who can forget the murder of one of our finest, Lieutenant Andrew Dailey." Zengo looked at his mother. The image of her father brought tears to her eyes every time the commercial aired. When the camera was back on McGovern, he held up a mug shot of Pandini Sr. "Ask yourself—do you really want to hand over the reins of the city to this man's son?"

Mrs. Zengo dabbed at her eyes with a napkin. Zengo patted her hand. "I just don't see how you can work for that man, Ricky!" she said.

Zengo's dad had his bill buried in the morning newspaper. "Those lousy reporters!" said his dad, neatly folding his paper and placing it on the kitchen table. Zengo spotted the article he had been reading—it was the one about his failure to protect Pandini. "Don't let them get to you. That story was rubbish."

Zengo let out a breath. He was glad his father felt that way. "Mom and Dad, you can be sure I've got my eyes open. But I'm really trying to keep an open mind about Mr. Pandini, at least while I'm reporting to his headquarters every day."

Zengo's dad took a sip of his coffee. "That's quite admirable, Rick. They say 'the apple doesn't fall far from the tree' . . . but sometimes that apple can roll down the hill and grow a whole new tree of its own. Speaking of which . . ."

At the sound of this, Zengo's mother stopped wiping down the countertop, poured herself a cup of coffee, and sat down at the kitchen table next to her husband.

Zengo looked between his parents. “What is it?”

“Well, your mom and I were thinking . . .”

Zengo’s mother placed her webbed hand on her husband’s back.

“Now that you have a job, it might be time for you to . . . branch out as well? You know, get your own place?”

Zengo almost choked on his toast. Move out? Sure, his parents annoyed him at times, but his mom knew just how he liked his toast. She greeted him with a freshly brewed hot chocolate every morning. Zengo thought of the clown mug he had stuck in the back of the cabinet his first day on the squad. He suddenly missed it.

“Right, of course,” he said. But where would he go?

"Oh, Ricky, this doesn't mean we don't want to see you anymore," his mother began.

"Oh, I know that, Mom," he said. And he did know that. But he had gotten so comfortable in his routine here.

"We knew you'd understand, Ricky," said his dad. "Remember, we can't really fly until we leave the nest."

Zengo nodded. So his father did think he had some growing to do. Zengo placed his hand on the Platypus Police Squad badge that hung around his neck. The metal was cold.

"I'd better get going," he said as he gulped down the last of his orange juice. "I want to stop at the station before I head over to Pandini Towers."

"Oh, Ricky, we are just so proud of you."

"Thanks, Mom," he said as he threw on his lucky leather jacket. His mom handed him his hot chocolate in a to-go mug, and he darted out the front door. He took a deep breath. Yes, he did have some growing to do. With every passing day, he learned more about what it took to be a good cop. Yesterday was a rough day, but today could only get better. He had a job to do. And he was going to prove to everyone that he could do it, all on his own.

PANDINI ENTERPRISES, 8:00 A.M.

After a briefing with the team back at Platypus Police Squad headquarters, Zengo arrived at Pandini Towers and was whisked past security to a VIP elevator, which shot him straight to the top floor. The elevator doors slid open to reveal Bobby, who escorted Zengo into the main room. Pandini looked up from the paperwork on his desk and greeted the detective. "Good morning, Rick." The sun was still rising above Kalamazoo City—the view was even more breathtaking in daylight hours.

Zengo nodded. "Mr. Pandini." He noticed that the

candidate had increased his security detail. In addition to Bobby, who remained by the elevator, there was a ferret prowling the perimeter of the suite, and, circling the ceiling, there were three seagulls, one wearing an eye patch. *Guess it couldn't help to have more eyes on the scene*, thought Zengo.

"I'm sorry that I wasn't there to foil the attack yesterday. I—"

Pandini put out his hand to silence the detective.

"Nonsense. You clipped the jerk's wing. You did what you could and I appreciate it. We're that much closer to bringing this guy to justice." Pandini continued to sign the paperwork and then handed the stack to a staffer who brought it to the next room.

"To help me do my job better, I need to ask you a few questions," said Zengo.

"I'm an open book," replied Pandini.

"Have you done anything in recent months to anger anyone? Does anyone on your payroll have any sort of"—Zengo looked around the room and lowered his voice—"grudge?"

"Detective, I'm a businessman and, now, a politician. I can't breathe without someone getting irritated. But I have no reason to believe that any of my actions in recent months has warranted such attacks, and I can't think of anyone who would have cause to do this. As I hope you have seen firsthand, I treat everyone with respect. I can only guess that whoever is perpetrating these attacks is holding a grudge left over from my father's era."

The bell at the elevator dinged and the doors slid open to reveal Irving Myers. "Frank, the morning poll numbers are in, and we are looking good!" Myers strode across the room, threw his briefcase on Pandini's desk, and opened it. He held up a stack of papers, each with a different set of graphs.

Pandini sat back in his chair. "That's wonderful news," he said with a subdued smile.

"You're up ten points from just a few days ago," the strategist said excitedly.

"Well, I'm glad that people are responding to my message."

The voice of Pandini's office manager rang through the phone speaker on his desk. "Mr. Pandini, call for you on line one. It's Patrick McGovern." Pandini and Myers shared a look. Pandini cocked an eyebrow.

"Thank you, Candace," he said, then picked up the receiver and, with a quick glance at Myers, tapped a

button, picking up the call and putting it on speaker.

"Good morning, Pat."

"Frank, my old friend. I am calling to offer you my best wishes. What terrible news to come out of your campaign in the last few days. I'm just calling to make sure you're all right."

Friend? thought Zengo. Is this the same guy who Zengo had just watched tear Pandini apart in a commercial this morning? Though he had to admit, McGovern did sound much more sincere than he did in his ads.

"Well, I appreciate the well wishes, Pat," said Pandini. "But you know me—it's going to take more than a couple of errant boomerangs to stop me. You're going to have to be on your toes in the upcoming debate."

"You mean like you were at the Branbury Prep homecoming dance?" McGovern laughed.

Pandini chuckled too. "Well, there's at least one embarrassing piece of my past you haven't dug up for those ads of yours."

"All's fair, Frank, my boy. You've known me a long time, long enough to know that I'd do anything for Kalamazoo."

"We still have something in common, then. Take care of yourself, Pat. See you at the debate." Pandini replaced the headset on the receiver.

"He's feeling the pressure," said Myers happily. "I can tell." Humming to himself and gathering his charts, he left the room.

"I know what you're thinking," Pandini said before Zengo could open his bill. He grinned sadly and shook his head. "It's not McGovern who's behind these attacks, I promise you."

"But Mr. Pandini," Zengo began, "he has the motive, and I bet he has the means. In my opinion, I think it's worth the other detectives giving him a very close look."

"I've known Patrick all my life," said Pandini. "He was the only one of my old friends who stuck by me when my father went to jail. We even went to college together—I studied business and Patrick studied law. We always told each other we'd come back to Kalamazoo City and work together to make it a better place—I would start successful businesses to make the economy strong, and Patrick would become district attorney to keep the city clean."

"So how come you're running against each other?" asked Zengo. "And why is he saying such mean things about you in his ads?"

"I don't know," said Pandini. "If I had to guess, I'd venture that he thinks I've been spending the last few years catering only to the rich and powerful. Of course, you and I know that nothing could be further from the truth, but it's been a long time since I've talked to Pat the way he and I did just now—not since Bamboo opened, that's for sure. I would like to think that if I were in his position I'd be kinder, but it's hard to tell for sure, isn't it?

"In any event," Pandini continued, "I know that Patrick McGovern would never do anything to truly hurt me. That is not in his nature. And those attack ads don't count. Like Pat said, it's just politics."

Zengo wasn't completely convinced. But he could

see that Pandini wanted him to drop this theory. "Okay," he said. "I'll try to look at it your way from now on."

"You do that," said Pandini, smiling. "We'll get to the bottom of this little crime spree, and then we'll go on and win the election!"

Myers came back in with more paperwork, but Pandini's phone buzzed again. "It's Jacob Nutter, line two," said his receptionist over the intercom.

Pandini picked up the handset this time to take the call. Not wanting to hover over Pandini, Zengo crossed to the windows in the large, open office. He looked down to the city streets.

Somewhere down there O'Malley was cruising around with his new partner. Zengo knew his job was important, but sitting there with Pandini as he took his phone calls, he started to feel like a glorified babysitter. All the talk of graphs, polls, inventories, bottom lines—it all sounded like a foreign language to Zengo.

Pandini suddenly raised his voice. Zengo's ears perked up. "I am sorry that you feel that way, Jacob. Yes, I know we have been in business for years, and I greatly value our partnership, but times are changing, and nut allergies just present too much of a risk—I can't abide the chance of another child being rushed to Kalamazoo Memorial Hospital from one of my restaurants again. We had this same conversation last week, and I have not changed my position. I know what an important part of Kalamazoo's economy Nutter's Nuts presents. But I won't put my patrons, or this city, at risk." Zengo hadn't ever heard Pandini so agitated. His face grew redder as he listened to Mr. Nutter on the other end of the call. "Yes, I understand that, Jacob, but I'm still going to have to cancel my orders, now and in the future. And if that's how you feel, good luck to you, sir."

Pandini's nostrils flared as he hung up the phone. He took a deep breath and slammed his fist on the desk. He looked across the room to see that he had caught Zengo off guard.

"No decision is ever easy in my line of work," he said. "I've worked with the owner of Nutter's Nut Factory for years."

"That must have been a tough call," said Zengo.

"Business is full of tough calls." Pandini picked up the phone and asked his office manager to connect him with his fish supplier.

Zengo crossed over to the window, and thought

again of O'Malley and Cooper, cruising around in O'Malley's car. *If I can't check this out, someone should.* He slipped his phone out of his jeans pocket and texted his old partner.

KALAMAZOO CITY STREETS, DOWNTOWN, 9:20 A.M.

Detective Corey O'Malley steered the cruiser angrily through the streets toward Kalamazoo U. Plazinski had told him and Cooper to go back there to see if they could dig up any more clues about the assaults on Pandini. O'Malley was pretty sure the trail there was cold, but he didn't have any better ideas. For an instant, he wished Zengo were riding shotgun again. That crazy kid would probably have come up with some half-baked theory by now that just might lead to a break in the case.

He glanced over at his new partner, who was flipping through the case folder. Cooper's work habits were like his—methodical, slow and steady, by the book. He was better off teamed up with someone like her. A break would come, sooner or later. *Sooner,* he hoped.

He was stopped at a red light when his phone beeped. He slipped it out of his back pocket and flipped it open. It was from Zengo.

The light changed. "There's a text from Zengo," he said, passing the phone to Cooper before stepping on the gas. "What's on his mind?"

"Not much," said Cooper. "'Pandini says investigating McGovern is a dead end. Had argument with Nutter's Nuts exec.' Is he trying to give us a tip?"

O'Malley also wondered what to make of it. Zengo was in a tough spot, instructed to stick to Pandini like feathers on a duck. Was this some sort of signal?

"I wonder if the comment about Nutter's Nuts has something to do with Pandini's campaign pledge about nut allergies," said Cooper. "You know? How he's going to reduce the amount of nuts in his restaurants and then, if he wins, across the whole town?"

"The folks over at Nutter's must be none too

pleased," said O'Malley.

"Does that sound like a possible motive to you?"

O'Malley smiled and nodded at his partner. "Just might be," he said. "Shall we take a swing by there?"

"Sounds like a plan," said Cooper. "Except . . ."

"Except what?" said O'Malley, turning onto the ramp to the highway.

"If there is anything going on at Nutter's, the last thing we need would be for the culprits to see us sniffing around the place. And I wonder if we're jumping the gun by pointing the finger at a disgruntled vendor?"

"A vendor that sells nuts," said O'Malley. "Foraging and selling nuts is the backbone of the squirrel economy in this city, and Nutter's Nut Factory has been owned by the same family for generations. Pandini Enterprises runs nearly a quarter of all the restaurants in town. Losing his account is going to be devastating to the Nutter family."

"But does that make them potential assassins?"

"Of course not," said O'Malley. "But it's a big company, there're bound to be a few wing nuts. . . ."

NUTTER'S NUTS
TOUR TICKETS

NUTTER'S NUT FACTORY, 9:45 A.M.

O'Malley pulled into a visitor's parking space at Nutter's Nut Factory. Dark gray smoke billowed from rusty smokestacks, staining the clear blue sky. It was a much gloomier place than was suggested by the commercials featuring Professor Nutter, the goofy cartoon character who was the company's mascot. Professor Nutter sported goggles, a bushy mustache, wild hair, and a lab coat, and sang about how nutritious nuts were.

"So what's the plan?" asked O'Malley.

"We're going to go on the tour," said Cooper, pulling

out a bag from her briefcase. "But we're going in undercover. I happen to have a few items here that I picked up when we were casing the costume shops. I think 'Janice' and 'Buck' are going to enjoy learning about the fascinating peanut-butter-making process. No sense going in with boomerangs blazing when we're just on a recon mission. According to the Nutter website, the tour visits every department in the factory. We'll get a look at just about everybody who works here."

Cooper tipped over the bag and an array of costume pieces spilled out—wigs, glasses, hats, even a fake mustache.

O'Malley liked this idea—a lot. He grabbed a mullet wig that came with large, pork-chop sideburns. He pulled it on over his big head. "'Buck,' reporting for duty. Let's do this!"

They quickly donned the rest of their disguises, and "Janice" and "Buck" were soon at a ticket counter splashed with the Nutter's Nuts logo.

"Welcome to Nutter's Nut Factory—home of Kalamazoo City's famous salted nuts and our award-winning peanut butter," said the cheerful ticket vendor. O'Malley thought she was unusually peppy, considering she was a very old squirrel. Probably been giving this greeting her entire life. He was impressed that she kept a straight face at the sight of their ridiculous getups. In addition to the mullet wig, O'Malley wore a fake goatee, a sleeveless T-shirt, jeans, and cowboy boots. Cooper wore a wig that towered a few feet above the top of her head and a purple velvet sweat suit.

"Hiya," said O'Malley. "Me and Janice are here for one of them factory tours."

"Wonderful!" said the greeter. "We have a tour leaving in just a moment." She gestured toward the group of schoolchildren bouncing around excitedly in the waiting room. There were at least twenty six-year-olds who couldn't contain their enthusiasm. They looked as though they might explode.

"Super," said Cooper. One of the children threw a rubber ball against the wall, and it bounced off, zooming straight toward Cooper's wig. Barely looking in the ball's direction, Cooper swiftly lifted her webbed hand and caught it.

"Evan McCallister!" scolded the teacher. "You say you're sorry to that nice lady!"

The boy sheepishly approached Cooper and

muttered an apology. She tossed the ball back and said, “Don’t worry about it, kid.” O’Malley was impressed by Cooper’s reaction speed. Had that been him, he’d probably be nursing a bump on his noggin.

The door marked “Tour Entrance” swung open. Out popped an oversize squirrel in a hard hat. He had the same markings as the receptionist, and by the looks of him, he was probably the factory’s single largest peanut butter consumer.

"WHO'S READY TO GO NUTS?" he hollered. The schoolchildren jumped up and down giddily and cheered.

"I'm Gerald, and I'll be your tour guide today! You each get to wear your very own hard hat!" The children cheered even louder as he handed out construction helmets with the Nutter's Nuts logo on them.

O'Malley and Cooper joined the group tour. And O'Malley had to admit it—he was kind of excited to see how peanut butter was made.

Gerald explained the process. "Mountains of nuts are taken from the giant silo at the center of the room. They are shelled individually by teams of experts."

Cooper and O'Malley watched as an army of squirrels cracked nuts and then put them on conveyor belts. Overhead, flying squirrels were gliding between catwalks.

“This place is lousy with squirrels,” said Cooper as they passed a loading bay.

“You got that right,” said O’Malley. He wriggled. “Kinda makes me feel . . . squirrely.”

He had evidently spoken a little too loudly. He realized this as a bushy-tailed squirrel with black spots strutted past, pushing a hand truck. The spotted squirrel gave him a dirty look.

“Sorry,” said O’Malley.

The squirrel gave an annoyed sniff and walked onward, blending almost instantly into the mad crush of workers on the factory floor.

"I have a feeling we might be in the right place," whispered O'Malley. "But there sure are a lot of possible suspects."

"How are we going to know which one is the culprit?" asked Cooper. "That is, if the culprit is even here?"

They turned their attention back to the tour, where Gerald was proudly gesticulating as he pointed to all the specialized equipment. "Our state-of-the-art sorting system separates the nuts and sends them into one of two directions—either to be salted and canned or mashed and turned into peanut butter!"

Must be backbreaking work, thought O'Malley.

Cooper whispered to O'Malley, "I wonder if any of them know that their jobs are about to get cut?"

O'Malley nodded and muttered, "If so, they might

be pretty desperate. And desperate people take desperate measures."

"Any questions?" asked Gerald, looking right at Cooper and O'Malley, his big, wide grin starting to fade. *Either he doesn't like folks chatting while he's giving a tour,* thought O'Malley, *or he's onto us.*

"Buck here and I were just wondering: How many nuts get shelled in an hour?" asked Cooper without missing a beat. "We have tried to shell our own nuts at home and man, lemme tell you—it ain't easy. I'm just so impressed with how quickly your employees shell them nuts!"

O'Malley smiled and nodded. It was a good save on his partner's part.

"Well, I'm proud to tell you that almost a quarter of a million nuts are shelled every hour of the day. We are the number-one supplier of nuts for the entire KC metro area!" Gerald turned to the kids. "Now, who wants to go check out the peanut butter mixer!" Unsurprisingly, they all jumped up and down and cheered.

NUTTER'S PEANUT BUTTER PROCESSING CENTER, 10:30 A.M.

"Nutter's Nuts is proud to bring you the creamiest, richest peanut butter! That is—unless you prefer chunky. We have that, too!" Gerald, chipper as ever, gave the tour a chuckle. "From our factory to your sandwich! We are one of the nation's leading innovators in peanut butter technology!"

Cooper and O'Malley were now standing with the schoolchildren in a massive room where shelled peanuts from the adjacent room traveled via conveyor belts in a dizzying configuration. The scent of peanuts was overpowering. And both detectives were scanning the scene in every direction, wondering which of the countless squirrels they saw around them—if any of them—might have been the perpetrator. With so many squirrels to choose from, how would they ever figure out if there was a suspect in their midst?

"Come!" Gerald beckoned. "We can watch from the observation deck! The nuts are about to get ground up and turned into that sweet, delicious goop we all love!" Gerald smacked his lips so loudly his head mike popped. He directed the group to a metal staircase that led up to a catwalk overlooking the operation.

The peanuts made their way up a ramp and onto a flat surface. The nuts were rhythmically pulverized with mallets that looked like giant meat tenderizers, to make them ready to mix.

Smoke billowed out of the top of the contraption with every compression. What was left of the nuts was almost a powder. This continued to journey on the conveyor belts, which ended at a giant mixing bowl. There, oil and sugar poured forth from tubes above. Then, an alarm rang out and giant mixing blades descended from the ceiling. "This is where you all will want to stand back!" yelled Gerald.

The whirring of the blades filled the room with a bit of a gust until they sunk into the ingredients.

O'Malley wasn't paying attention, though. He was too busy trying to keep track of every squirrel he saw. It wasn't easy. He wished he had a bit of Zengo's sixth sense for spotting criminals. What would Zengo notice that was escaping O'Malley? He thought back to the gawky squirrel with the dolly back at the loading bay who had eyeballed them earlier. He had seemed suspicious. But maybe he was just curious.

"I keep thinking about that little creep with the hand truck," O'Malley whispered to Cooper, his mouth barely moving, after first making sure that Gerald was distracted. He did not want to be the target of another hairy eyeball from the guide.

"You mean that guy?" whispered Cooper.

O'Malley was startled. What was the spotted squirrel doing here, clear over on the other side of the factory from where they had first seen him? Was it the same guy? O'Malley squinted to make sure. The squirrel's tail was spotted—just like the other one. And he seemed to be watching the tour group out of the corner of his eye. Or was that just O'Malley's imagination? This was by far the hardest thing about the job.

O'Malley decided to do his best to keep an eye on the squirrel while pretending to be completely fascinated with the peanut-butter-making process. This was not easy. He was no actor. He knew four eyes were better than two, so he pulled Cooper to the back of the tour crowd to share his suspicions.

"What makes you so sure?" she asked.

Though O'Malley hated to admit it, he did not have much to go on. "A hunch?" he said.

Cooper looked back at him skeptically. "Okay," she said with a shrug. "I'll try to keep an eye on him. You do the same. Why don't we split up and each go to one edge of the group. We can pretend we're each checking out a different part of the process."

Now Cooper too was on full alert. Soon, she signaled O'Malley and pointed to a bushy tail, covered in black spots, sticking out from behind a barrel by the exit. The markings were unmistakable. It had to be the same squirrel yet again. Why was he shadowing them?

O'Malley looked away, and when he looked back again, the squirrel was gone.

"That's it," he said, breaking away from the group to go after him, but Cooper grabbed his arm.

"Stop!" she whispered fiercely. "Don't blow our cover! He's not even a flying squirrel!"

"He knows something!" whispered O'Malley. "I can tell!"

An instant later, a ball bounced past Cooper's feet.

"My ball!" shouted Evan McCallister, the trouble-making kid from the waiting room. The ball bounced right off the observation deck and into the vat of peanut butter, where the mixing blades were now rotating at a dizzying speed. And the boy was running right after it.

"STOP!" shouted Gerald, running toward the boy. Cooper ran toward the kid, too. But they were both too late. The boy lost his footing and fell off the platform, his arms flailing helplessly as he fell with a splat into the mixing bowl. Cooper didn't hesitate. She leaped off the platform like an Olympic diver, sailing through the air, her beehive wig blowing off as she did. She landed with a plop in the sticky brown vat of goop, right next to the boy. As they struggled to stay above

the surface in the swirling sea of peanut butter, she reached for his arm and pulled him close to her.

Gerald fumbled with his walkie-talkie and yelled, "CODE RED! CODE RED!" The sound of machines slowing to a halt left only the sounds of the screaming students and the chaperones who feared for the boy's life.

But Evan McCallister was in good hands—Jo Cooper's. She safely kept the boy afloat and maneuvered past the mixing blades each time they approached. As soon as the mixing bowl came to a complete stop, she lifted him to the emergency workers, who carried him to safety via a cherry-picker truck.

O'Malley cringed. Would strands of Cooper's wig end up in some kids' sandwiches?

He looked over and spied the spotted squirrel again. This time, he didn't take his eyes off him, and the squirrel took off toward an area of the factory marked "DANGER—OFF-LIMITS."

Having confidence that Cooper would handle the situation with the boy, O'Malley slid down the railing of the catwalk staircase and gave chase. He was certain the squirrel had kicked the boy's ball out of his hand and into the peanut butter. A clever distraction, but not clever enough. "Cooper! Come in, Cooper!" She radioed back, but her voice was muffled. O'Malley couldn't hear what she was saying; he was just glad that she wasn't over her head in peanut butter.

O'Malley put his radio away and rushed through the maze of pipes and barrels that littered the Nutter's Nuts Factory floor, careful to not lose sight of the spot-tailed assailant.

Employees were scattering in every direction. The suspect jumped up to a ladder that was on the side of the supply silo and scaled the wall at a pace faster than O'Malley could keep up with. The detective withdrew his boomerang and shouted, "Platypus

Police Squad! FREEZE!" The squirrel didn't even look back, but continued to climb upward. O'Malley took a deep breath. He aimed just above the fleeing squirrel. The boomerang struck the supply tower and created a gaping hole, which sent nuts shooting out. O'Malley ducked for cover underneath the conveyor belt as nuts continued to spew, bringing the squirrel down with it. The rumbling sound of the avalanche was deafening.

O'Malley dug his way out of the rubble, but he was too late. The squirrel had chewed his way out faster. The squirrel pushed past the other factory workers toward the end of the room. As he swung open the emergency-exit door, he looked back at O'Malley and grinned.

But Jo Cooper was waiting for him on the other side of the door. She socked him across the muzzle

and jumped on top of him, pulled his arms behind his back, and cuffed him.

"You have the right to remain silent," she began.

PLATYPUS POLICE SQUAD HEADQUARTERS, 6:10 P.M.

The squirrel fidgeted in his seat. The chair wasn't designed to be comfortable. It wasn't even built for his size—his head barely made it to the top of the table. The room was dark, the only light cast by a single lamp that hung down from the ceiling over the table. It was quiet—except for the sound of a ticking clock.

A door hinge squeaked. In walked Detectives O'Malley and Cooper.

"So . . . whoever you are," said O'Malley.

The squirrel did not look up.

"You think you're pretty clever, withholding your name," O'Malley continued. "But we have ways of making you talk. And once we run your paw prints through the system, I'm willing to bet we'll be able to ID you. Even though you're nothing more than a punk kid, I don't think this is your first time in a police station."

The squirrel did not look up.

"What I particularly want to know," said O'Malley, getting right in the squirrel's face, "is what you've been up to this past week. Specifically, where were you two nights ago . . . and yesterday evening?"

The squirrel leaned on his fist and mumbled something.

"What was that, punk?" said O'Malley. "I couldn't HEAR you."

"Like I'm gonna tell you," sneered the squirrel.

A loud popping sound made both O'Malley and the squirrel look up. It was Cooper, cracking her knuckles. As though she was getting ready to mean business with her fists. She eyed the suspect with a glare of steel. "There are ways to make you talk," she said in a voice of deadly calm. "And most of them aren't pretty."

"Not another word, A.J.!" shouted an all-too-familiar voice as the interrogation-room door burst open with a bang. It was Doug Raskin, Kalamazoo City's most notorious lawyer.

"Why should he start now?" asked Cooper cuttingly. "Glad you're here, Raskin. Maybe you can persuade your client to open his mouth."

"He has nothing to say!" said Raskin. "Your case has more holes than a fishing net! How dare you throw your boomerangs around at Nutter's Nuts Factory and then haul an innocent worker away?" He put a protective wing around the squirrel. "Come on. We're getting out of here. And I'm going to file an enormous lawsuit against the Platypus Police Squad."

O'Malley recovered quickly from this surprise.

"Raskin, maybe you can tell me how a factory worker can afford a high-priced lawyer like you? I bet he doesn't make enough in a year to cover the down payment on the new car you drove into our lot."

Raskin glared and pulled the squirrel's chair back. "You leave my car out of this," he said fiercely.

But O'Malley wasn't going to be sidetracked. "Are you going to tell us who really hired you?"

"*I* hired Mr. Raskin," said a furious voice. In walked a squirrel with wild gray hair and a mustache. He was tall—well, tall for a squirrel—and wore goggles and a lab coat.

"Professor Nutter, I don't know what you're doing here, but this is official police business," said O'Malley.

"Professor Nutter? That is a made-up character! I am Jacob Nutter! The president of Nutter's Nuts Factory! How *dare* you arrest my grandson!"

Plazinski was hot on Nutter's heels, his angry vein popping way out on his forehead.

Hoo boy. O'Malley had to pull himself together. Nervously, he tucked in that part of his shirt that always popped out and stood up straight. In spite of the tense situation, he gave a nervous laugh. He couldn't believe how much the real Mr. Nutter looked a whole lot like the crazy cartoon mascot.

Plazinski glared at the detective. "There is nothing funny going on here, O'Malley. You better have a dang good explanation as to why you arrested A. J. Nutter."

"Um . . . the perpetrator . . . I mean, the *suspect* here . . ." He indicated A.J., who had replaced his sullen expression with a smirk. "He was acting quite shifty when we saw him at the factory. We kept catching him staring at us. So, naturally, we began to watch him as well. We are charged with trying to find the criminal who twice made an attempt on the life of Frank Pandini. And after we were tipped off that Pandini had canceled a big contract with your factory . . . we thought there might be a motive. So we were investigating. And your grandson's behavior was beyond suspicious."

"Who told you that Pandini canceled a contract with us?" said Mr. Nutter. "That is privileged information. And in any case, there's a big difference between being upset at a business deal falling through and ordering an attack on someone!"

"Besides," said Raskin, "didn't I see on TV that the assailants were reportedly flying squirrels?" He indicated A.J.'s skinny little squirrel arms. "Look for yourself! This kid can't glide!"

"Yeah," said A.J., "and I ain't never worked a catering job in my life, neither."

Plazinski had heard enough. "Please accept our apologies, Mr. Nutter. A.J., you are free to go. I can promise you that both of these detectives will be reprimanded."

Raskin and Mr. Nutter lifted A.J. from his chair by the elbows and hustled him out of the room. "Ta-ta!" said Raskin over his shoulder.

As soon as they left, Plazinski laced into O'Malley and Cooper. "What were you thinking, arresting

someone without a shred of evidence? And of all people, the grandson of one of the most prominent people in town! Have you lost your minds?"

"We had ample cause," said Cooper. "I saw A.J. pull a move that put a small child's life at risk. The kid might have drowned in peanut butter!"

O'Malley glanced gratefully at his partner. "Besides," he added, "we found out that the perp we are looking for was only disguised as a flying squirrel. Zengo hit the assailant in the wing with a boomerang at KCU and nothing happened. He was wearing fake gliders."

Plazinski was not convinced. "Even so, that doesn't prove that anyone at Nutter's Nuts was involved. What other leads do you have?"

O'Malley and Cooper looked at each other. "That was our only lead, Sergeant," said O'Malley.

"Well, you better get another one, quick!" said Plazinski. "This case is going nowhere, and we're all going to be sent back to walking the beat if there's another attempt on Pandini." He stalked off to his office, probably to throw a few things.

O'Malley turned to his partner. "Thanks for having my back there, Cooper."

"You know, I thought you were making a big mistake, going after that little squirt in the factory . . ." said Cooper.

"I know, but—" said O'Malley.

Cooper cut him off. "What I'm saying is, I thought you were wrong at the time, but I don't anymore. A.J. said that he's never had a catering job in his life. How did he know that the squirrel who attacked Pandini at his penthouse was dressed as a member of the catering staff? Nobody knew about that except for the few people who were there."

"That's right," said O'Malley, relieved and excited that Cooper was with him on this one. "That kid knows something. I feel it in my bones."

"I'd be willing to bet someone at Nutter's Nuts is behind these attacks."

O'Malley pondered the situation. There was no way they could get back inside the factory to dig up more information. But there must be some other angle.

"We need to talk to Zengo," he said.

PANDINI CAMPAIGN HEADQUARTERS, 7:15 A.M.

Zengo's day with Pandini started early. He monitored the tycoon's endless morning phone meetings, marveling at the way in which Pandini could go from one call to another without missing a beat. Zengo was exhausted just watching.

Following Pandini around was even more tiring. The tycoon liked to visit each of his business enterprises every day, and he had campaign stops to make too. And everywhere the panda went, the press was sure to go. They hounded him relentlessly. Pandini dealt with each rude intrusion with his usual combination of charm and misdirection. But they swarmed him like sharks, always hungry for more.

Finally, it was obvious that Pandini had had enough. He winked at Zengo as they entered his club Bamboo, not yet open for the day. Once behind the main door, Pandini locked it. "Come with me," he said. "We're going out the back way. And we're going to visit an old friend of mine."

Pandini seemed to have cars and drivers at his command. One was waiting for them at the back door of the club. They hopped inside. Carpy was at the wheel. "To Frank's!" said Pandini.

Zengo thought they'd be heading to the nearest hot dog stand. But instead, they went way down to the oldest part of town, to the original Frank's Franks. It was a proud local institution—a little battered and beat, but as much a part of Kalamazoo City as Town Hall or Founder's Rock, and the original model for the Frank's Franks stands that had popped up around town.

Here, they went in the back way and entered the kitchen. There was an old-timer manning the grill. He looked up and beamed. "Howdy, Frank!" said Pandini. "How are the dogs rolling?"

Zengo was astounded. He had no idea there was

still an actual Frank at Frank's. He was looking at a living legend.

"Hey there, Mr. Pandini!" said Frank.

"Now, now, please call me Frank, Frank!" said Pandini. He proudly gestured around the grill station and glanced at Zengo. "Isn't this place the best?" He took a big sniff. "Just smell those frankfurters!"

Zengo had to admit the dogs at the original Frank's Franks did smell pretty fantastic. Even though it was only mid-morning, he felt his stomach growl.

Frank looked at Zengo. He could spot a customer at a hundred paces. "How about if I fix you up a footlong with extra onions?" he said.

Zengo started to protest. He hadn't eaten an actual meat hot dog since he was a kid. But he could see that Frank would not be denied. Zengo accepted the juicy concoction with both hands. Before he knew it, he had swallowed half of it. "This is . . . delicious!" he said, his mouth full.

Pandini said, "Another satisfied customer."

Frank beamed.

"You know, when I bought this business, I wasn't just trying to find another way to make a buck," said Pandini to Zengo. "I've been coming here my whole life.

Nobody, but nobody, delivers a hot dog like Frank. I wanted to give him the chance to share his genius with a bigger audience. This here's the original operation—and it's the place where we take all the Frank's Franks cooks to learn hot dog making from a master."

"Mr. Pandini saved my bacon a few years back," said Frank to Zengo. "I was about to go out of business. I had started to think people just didn't like hot dogs anymore."

"Nonsense!" said Pandini. "They just needed to be greeted by the irresistible smell of Frank's Franks, no matter where they were in the city!"

While they were talking, Zengo had been trying to eat the second half of his hot dog as slowly as possible. It was the best thing he had ever put into his mouth, and he never wanted it to end. No wonder O'Malley was so crazy for this place. "That was incredible," he said to Frank, who smiled and handed him another. Why not? He'd be sure to eat an extra-healthy dinner.

With a fond farewell, Pandini and Zengo left Frank's Franks and headed back to Bamboo. Once more, they went in the back door and outfoxed the ravenous reporters. Up in Pandini's office they found a flustered Irving Myers.

"Take a look at this new ad from McGovern," he said. He clicked the remote and a flat-screen television lowered from the ceiling.

Patrick McGovern appeared before the Kalamazoo City skyline. "We live in a great city," said McGovern. "A great city filled with great people—and great businesses. There is nothing more important than keeping the businesses in this city humming. As mayor, I promise to do that for you. A good economy makes a great city."

The scene changed. Now McGovern was standing in front of Nutter's Nut Factory at closing time, hundreds of squirrels streaming out. "Nutter's Nuts is one of the most important pieces in Kalamazoo City's economy. It is a flagship employer in our fair city, and has been for years. My mother, Alice, raised me on her own on her Nutter's Nuts salary. And what do you think Frank Pandini Jr. would like to do with this important enterprise?" The scene shifted again. Through clever use of computer graphics, the factory appeared closed, shuttered, out of business.

"That's right, fellow citizens. Frank Pandini wants to drive this fine company out of business and put all its hard workers on the bread line. And once that happens, all the small companies will follow suit—if the workers are on the street, how will the shoemaker make a living? The corner grocery? The barbershop? I promise you, that will *never* happen on my watch. In my administration we will do everything we can to keep Kalamazoo City strong and its businesses growing.

"A vote for me, Patrick McGovern, is a vote for a great future for Kalamazoo City!"

Irving Myers clicked off the television and started walking around in a nervous circle. Pandini just kept shaking his head back and forth.

Zengo was furious. "This is so unfair! You're trying to keep schools and restaurants safe for kids with nut allergies! And how can McGovern claim that you don't care about small businesses! Look at what you've done for Frank's Franks!"

Pandini smiled sadly and sighed. "He's just trying to win an election. I hope I never have to stoop so low myself."

Myers was gnawing on his fist. "The average KC citizen will eat this ad up. We have to absolutely nail the debate tonight. The polls are rocky as it is. If you don't come through with a definite win, we're sunk."

"I was going to talk to you about that debate," said Zengo. "I'm a little worried about us letting Pandini step out in front of the public again after what's gone on the past few days. Especially since we have no idea who is behind this threat."

Myers circled back to face Zengo. "That is what you are supposed to be taking care of—Pandini's safety.

Why don't you actually do your job and leave the campaign decisions to us!"

Zengo started to fire back himself, but Pandini put up a hand. "Irving is right, Rick," he said. "We've got to see this through." He turned to Myers. "And I don't want you to worry about the polls. We'll be fine."

Myers was not comforted. "Maybe you aren't going to worry about the numbers, but I am!" he said. "And I'd like to take some time right now to go over strategy."

Pandini sat down at his desk and motioned for Myers to take a seat. Myers looked around at Zengo. "Alone—okay, chief?"

Chief. They were treating him just like the people down at the station. He looked to Pandini, but he just shrugged at Zengo and said, "Why don't you take a break for a bit, Rick?"

Zengo eyed Myers with suspicion. What was his game plan? Did he have more than just his reputation at stake in this election? Reluctantly, he stepped outside.

Just as he did, his phone vibrated. It was O'Malley. Just what he needed—someone else who always treated him like a kid.

"Hey," said Zengo. "What do you want?"

“To see you, sooner rather than later,” said O’Malley. “We thought we had a hot lead on the case. We even arrested a suspect—A. J. Nutter, Jacob Nutter’s grandson. Plazinski made us release him—lack of evidence—but we think there’s a thread here worth pulling. Can you meet up?”

“As it happens, I do have some free time,” said Zengo, more than a little curious.

They made a plan to meet at Mulligan’s, just down the street from Bamboo. Probably not a coincidence that it was O’Malley’s favorite greasy spoon.

BRENDA

MULLIGAN'S RESTAURANT, 4:10 P.M.

Zengo got there first and sat in the back-corner booth at Mulligan's restaurant, hidden behind a menu. Mulligan's was a dimly lit dump with no frills, but great food. It wasn't crowded just yet, but it soon would be. This was a popular spot for cops to meet up after work.

Zengo was eager to hear the story of the arrest of A. J. Nutter. But he figured that kid was just the tip of the iceberg. Pandini had plenty of enemies in and around Kalamazoo City. Whatever A.J.'s involvement, he wasn't working alone. Zengo wondered why

O'Malley was so eager to meet with him face-to-face. Did he genuinely need his help? Or did he maybe want to share a pile of Mulligan's famous onion rings with his old partner?

"Hey, look who it is," said a familiar voice. "Pandini's babysitter."

"Is it nap time?" said another.

Zengo looked up into the faces of Diaz and Lucinni. They were both grinning like idiots. *Not surprising—they* are *idiots*, thought Zengo.

"Hi, guys," he said, with a weary flap of his webbed fingers.

The door banged open and O'Malley came in, followed by Cooper.

"Fancy meeting you guys here," said Diaz.

"What is this?" asked Lucinni as he looked directly at Cooper. "A tea party?"

"Yeah," said Diaz. "Where's your tiara?"

Diaz and Lucinni laughed and smacked their webbed hands together in a high five.

Cooper stepped up to Lucinni and drew herself up to her full height, which still left quite a gap between the top of her head and the bottom of his bill. "Don't you have something better to do than mess with your fellow officers in the middle of a workday? Do I need to report you to the sergeant?"

Lucinni scowled at her. "You need to lighten up, little lady. And you need to get that chip off your shoulder." He made a move as though he was going to flick a real chip off her shoulder. But Cooper was far too quick for him. In one swift motion she took Lucinni down to the ground.

"And by the way, you knucklehead, I don't drink tea." She turned to Diaz. "And my partner left his tiara in the car." She released Lucinni and sat back down. The big oaf of a detective brought himself to his knees and caught his breath.

"Geez, it was just a joke!" he said, rubbing his wrists.

"Wasn't funny," said Cooper, standing up and dusting herself off. "Try me again when you've worked up a decent routine."

Diaz and Lucinni stomped out.

"Nobody messes with my partner," O'Malley shouted after them, a grin on his face.

At first Zengo thought O'Malley was sticking up for him, but then he remembered—Cooper was his partner now. They slid into the booth opposite Zengo.

"Nice to see you," said Zengo, looking only at O'Malley. Even though he knew he was being immature, he could not hide the fact that he wished his old partner had come on his own.

"Nice to see you, too," said Cooper, equally pointedly.

There was obviously no sense in acting like Cooper wasn't there. Zengo decided to take another approach.

He nodded at her and said, "You're welcome."

"For what?" said Cooper.

"For the tip about Nutter's Nuts," said Zengo. "And Cooper, congratulations on your first arrest with the Platypus Police Squad. You've got to admit you would never have run into this angle sitting behind a desk and following 'procedures,'" said Zengo, making air quotes on the last word.

Cooper rolled her eyes and folded her arms tightly. She turned away from Zengo and started tapping her foot angrily.

Zengo smirked. He couldn't help it. He was glad he had gotten under her skin.

"Come on, you guys!" said O'Malley. "If we expect to solve this case, we need to work together as a team."

Cooper rolled her eyes again. But then she looked Zengo square in the face. "Look. Your tip put a crack in this case, but it didn't split it wide-open. And now the Nutter family knows we're snooping around their business."

"We need to know if you've seen anything unusual within Pandini's operation," said O'Malley. "Whose tail is Pandini stepping on?"

Before Zengo could answer, Big Brenda, the

well-known waitress at the joint, interrupted their conversation. “What can I get for yah?” she asked.

O’Malley ordered for the table. “Three root beer floats and a jumbo basket of onion rings.”

“You’ve got it, sweetie,” she said, jotting the order down on her notepad.

“Thanks, Brenda.”

She was barely out of earshot when Zengo said, “You just can’t help but be in charge, can you?”

“Did I order anything you didn’t like?” asked O’Malley.

“No,” admitted Zengo.

"Then quit your complaining!" barked O'Malley. "And let us know what you've got."

"Pandini is surrounded by a passionate support base. Anyone he has ever helped is doing everything they can to help get him elected. This thing runs deeper than politics. I'm not convinced we're just looking for an enemy of his here."

"Interesting," said O'Malley. "Could someone close to Pandini be behind the attacks?"

"When it comes to Pandini, everyone's a suspect," said Cooper. "He doesn't surround himself with the most trustworthy people."

"Hold on now—" said Zengo.

"Think about what's gone on in KC in the past few years. The fish caper—one of Pandini's crew was behind it. And the whole fiasco at the Disaster Dome? The takedown of the former mayor?"

"You can't pin that on Pandini," said Zengo.

"Not directly," said Cooper. "But he's always only one step away from the people being charged. There's no smoke without fire."

"Is there anybody in that crowd who strikes you as off base?" asked O'Malley.

In fact, there was someone Zengo had been

considering. “There is, actually. The campaign manager—Irving Myers. That guy has been a nervous wreck about Pandini’s poll numbers.”

“You think he might be staging these attacks to help Pandini get more support from voters?” said O’Malley.

“I’ve begun to wonder,” said Zengo.

“It’s a solid theory,” said Cooper. “But where’s the connection with Nutter’s Nuts?”

She had him there. “I don’t know,” he said. “It’s just a hunch right now.”

“That’s some hunch,” said Derek Dougherty. The chameleon was sitting in the next booth over, with his back to O’Malley and Cooper. The reporter had been eavesdropping on their entire conversation.

O’Malley turned and glared at him. “You have a lot of nerve,” he sneered.

"That's what makes me so good at my job," said Derek, smiling and puffing up his chest. "Couldn't help but overhear you mentioning Pandini's crew. . . . Perhaps you'll be interested in my new book." Derek handed O'Malley a thick hardcover. "It's fresh from the printers. It'll be available tomorrow, wherever books are sold."

Zengo read the title out loud. "*A City Under Siege: A History of the Scourge of Frank Pandini Sr.*"

"Lots of great archival photos in that from the *Krier*," said Derek, flipping to a page with a photo of a much younger O'Malley.

"Wow! You used to have hair!" said Cooper.

"And a perm?" scoffed Zengo.

"Hey! It was the times," said O'Malley. He deflected the attention back at Dougherty. "Capitalizing on the city's pain. Sounds just like you, Derek," said O'Malley.

Derek plucked the book out of O'Malley's hands. "There's an entire chapter about your grandfather, Detective Zengo."

Dougherty opened the book to the chapter on Lieutenant Dailey and plopped the book in front of Zengo. The detective flipped the book shut and shoved it across the table. No matter what was there, it would not dignify his grandfather's sacrifice or memory. Derek Dougherty was nothing more than a nosy hack. He had no right to tell Lieutenant Dailey's story. "My grandfather would be disgusted by your book, Dougherty," said Zengo.

"I don't know, Detective," said Dougherty. "I think he'd be more concerned about Platypus Police Squad being in Pandini Jr.'s pocket."

"Pandini is not his dad," Zengo shot back.

"My, my, my. Are you the same detective who once accused the candidate of running the illegal fish trade in the city?"

"I was wrong," said Zengo. "And you publishing this book while Pandini Jr. is really trying to do good in this city—stop trying to take him down just to sell books and newspapers."

"Well, we'll see how Pandini does tonight at the debate," said Derek. "My money is on McGovern. Pandini is a slick businessman who has done a great deal for this city—but you can't buy your way into City Hall. Hate to see such a public-spirited guy go down—but it would make for a good story." Dougherty jumped down from his booth and tipped his hat to the detectives. "Now, if you'll excuse me, I must get ready for my award-winning coverage of tonight's festivities. Detective Zengo, you go ahead and keep that book. Want me to sign it for you?"

Zengo made like he was going to swing a punch at Derek just to see him flinch. Derek predictably did so and then scurried off.

Big Brenda came by with their order balanced on a tray.

"Scumbag," huffed O'Malley.

Big Brenda put her hand on her hips. "There's a problem?"

"No, no! Not you . . ." O'Malley knew better than to have a problem with Big Brenda.

"I thought not," she said while plunking down a root beer float in front of each detective.

Cooper leafed through the pages of the book Derek had left behind. "Fascinating to see photos of what Kalamazoo City looked like back in the day. It's really been built up over the years."

"You like that book so much, you can keep it," said Zengo as he stood up and threw on his jacket.

"Where are you going?" asked O'Malley.

"I have to get to the debate," Zengo said, turning to leave.

"I thought that would have been postponed," said O'Malley.

"Nope," said Zengo. "I suggested it. But Pandini insists on going forward. I'm worried that since we haven't been able to nab anyone, he's more at risk tonight than ever."

As Zengo left Mulligan's he caught sight of the televisions mounted above the bar. Each was tuned to a different news program, all of them predicting a defeat for Pandini tonight. *He'd be ahead if anyone was willing to give him a fair shot*, thought Zengo.

$3
Today's Special

KALAMAZOO CITY UNIVERSITY, MAIN AUDITORIUM, 5:30 P.M.

When Zengo arrived backstage at Pandini's dressing room in the auditorium, the candidate was in the middle of having his makeup applied. Myers was with him, still very agitated. "Where have you been, Zengo?" asked Myers.

The detective didn't feel the need to answer. After all, Myers had basically tossed him out of Pandini's office not too long ago.

There was a knock at the dressing-room door. Zengo opened it and was surprised to see Patrick

McGovern. "May I help you?" said Zengo.

Pandini called, "Pat? Is that you?"

"I just came by to say that I wish you well today, Frank," said McGovern.

"You too," said Pandini.

Zengo thought he heard a slight edge of hurt in Pandini's tone. McGovern's ads must really sting.

"I just wanted to say it again," McGovern began, "this is just politics. You know we haven't always seen eye to eye, but I would never say anything about you that I wouldn't say straight to your face."

Pandini nodded. "I feel the same way."

"So let's go out there and show the voters that they have two good choices in this election."

"Sure," said Pandini. Then, regaining his usual cheer, he added, "As long as they know that one of these good choices is just a little better than the other!"

He gave a hearty chortle, and McGovern joined in, though a little less heartily.

Irving Myers's phone beeped just then and he excused himself. What was so important that he had to go take the call in private? Zengo figured Pandini was safe here with McGovern. He waited a moment and followed Myers out of the dressing room.

Irving had gone to a shadowy hallway at a far end

of the building. Zengo was able to follow him without being detected. He hid himself behind a door and peeked out. Myers was meeting with someone. Before his eyes adjusted to the light, Zengo was not sure who it was.

A moment later, though, he saw. Myers was talking to a squirrel.

The whole time they were talking, Myers was looking all around, as though to make sure they weren't being observed. Before he could be spotted, Zengo ducked behind the corner and headed back to the prep room. His hunch was turning into a real suspicion. And if Myers was behind these attacks, this certainly meant something was going to go down tonight.

THE STREETS OF KALAMAZOO CITY, 5:40 P.M.

"What was it like here, back in the day?" asked Cooper as she flipped through Derek Dougherty's book.

O'Malley was behind the wheel. He gazed out the window. "For one thing, you didn't see as many people walking around at night. Kalamazoo City wasn't a safe place."

"I wouldn't say it's a totally safe place at night now," said Cooper.

"Back then, you wouldn't dare step out after sundown. Not with Frank Pandini Sr. running this town."

"And you worked under Lieutenant Dailey?"

"He was one of the best," said O'Malley. "Heart of gold, spine of steel, that one had."

"Says here you were part of the final raid that took Pandini Sr. down," said Cooper. She had the book opened to a page that reprinted the cover of the *Kalamazoo City Krier* from the big arrest.

"Yeah—that was one of the scariest nights of my life," said O'Malley. "We had been running surveillance on Pandini's operations for over a year at that point. If we had dropped the ball that night, we'd have been done for. Pandini Sr. had his paws in everything that went down in the KC underworld, but there was nothing we could pin on him.

"Then we received intel that Pandini was about to receive a big shipment of contraband—illegal fish, stolen motorbikes, banned nuts. . . . It would have been the biggest influx of contraband in Kalamazoo history. If it made it into the streets, it would have put every honest merchant out of business and destroyed the economy of the city, while making Pandini even richer.

"It was raining that night, and the fog really hampered the operation. Dailey had brought me up from the academy—he was like a father to me. He chose me to be his right-hand man for the investigation, and I was at his side that night. That didn't go over too well with some of the cops who had hit the beat longer than I had."

"Like Plazinski?" Cooper asked.

"Yeah, how'd you know? Is that in the book?" O'Malley asked.

Cooper shrugged. "I'm sure Plazinski is in this book somewhere, but that just explains why he bosses you around the way he does."

"Huh," said O'Malley as he drove along. "Well, anyhow, yes, Plazinski was there that night. Dailey had us all planted throughout the docks. We each had our station, ready to pounce. And we had reason to believe that Pandini would be there himself that night. He was a smart man. Ordinarily he let his goons handle these sorts of deals so he could keep his paws clean. But the shipment that night was too big to trust to one of his cronies.

"Just after midnight, a large cruise ship pulled up to the dock that was closest to Dailey and me. It wasn't strange to have boats coming and going at that hour, but typically they were smaller fishing vessels. A cruise boat filled with tourists wouldn't pull up to shore in the nighttime unless there were problems aboard.

"For about an hour, there was no movement. Then we saw a set of headlights through the foggy night sky. Then a second set, then a third, and then a fourth. Evidently Pandini's team was bigger than we had expected. When all the cars got to the end of the dock, the doors started opening. Soon the dock was full of thugs. And right in the middle, there he was—Frank Pandini Sr."

"So then what happened?"

"We had to get proof that they were up to something illegal and not just out for a midnight stroll. Soon enough, cargo started unloading from the ship. And that's when Dailey stuck his neck out. He had to get a look in those containers before we made the collar, find out exactly what we were dealing with."

"So how did he do it?"

"He managed to climb up to the top of one of the cargo containers. Then, silently, he slipped into the access hatch, grabbed some of the cargo, and made it back to where the rest of us were hiding. He had enough evidence in his arms to land Pandini in the slammer. Now we just had to surprise them and round them up.

"On Dailey's cue, we all charged with boomerangs

in hand. But that didn't faze Pandini and his crew. They didn't even seem surprised to see us. They threw open their car doors, used them as shields. Then they pulled out their own boomerangs. Of course none of those were street legal—no permits at all.

"Per Dailey's instructions, we were to take Pandini alive. We wanted to make an example of him, show any would-be criminals that crime doesn't pay, not in Kalamazoo City. So we were concentrating our efforts on finding a way to sneak up on them from the rear. That was our mistake," he said, his voice a little shaky.

"What do you mean?" said Cooper.

"We didn't have enough men to properly flank

Pandini's forces," said O'Malley. "I was supposed to cover Lieutenant Dailey, but there were too many of them to handle. . . ." He stopped talking and sighed.

"So that's how Dailey went down?" said Cooper. "What happened next?"

"Pandini's limousine took off at a million miles an hour," said O'Malley.

"I left it to one of the other cops to get Dailey to the hospital. And after what had happened, I was not going to let that creep get away.

"I jumped behind the wheel of the squad

car. I never drove so fast in my life. Pandini's driver was a maniac—careening up on sidewalks, taking hairpin turns into the wrong direction on one-way streets. Finally, I had a clear enough shot. I pulled back and tossed my boomerang, taking out two of their tires. Pandini's car spun out of control and crashed into an abandoned warehouse.

"I rushed to the car. Everyone in it was alive. By then more backup had arrived. We rushed to pull everyone from the wreckage and carried them to safety before their car caught fire."

"And Pandini was put away for life?"

"Yup, he spent the rest of his life behind bars."

"And what about Dailey?" asked Cooper.

"He was wounded badly," said O'Malley, shaking his head. "But Dailey, he was determined. He made a full recovery, got back to work . . . only to meet his demise at the hands of one of the few hired thugs Pandini had left after the excitement of the trial quieted down. Even behind bars, Pandini's reach was long."

"At least Dailey died knowing Pandini had been put away for life," said Cooper. "And KC has been one of the safest cities in the country ever since.

Pandini might have gotten away if not for you. What a story."

O'Malley was a little embarrassed, but proud at the same time. "Even though we only worked together for a short time, we were a good team. A great team," he said. "If it had been longer, who knows what else we might have been able to do?"

Cooper examined photos from the crime scene that were republished in Dougherty's book. "O'Malley, what became of the captain of the cruise ship, the one who was working with Pandini Sr.?"

"He was thrown in jail with the lot of them."

"And his family?"

"No idea," said O'Malley.

"This boat, it's called the *Miss Alice McG*," said Cooper.

"So, what does that have to do with anything?" asked O'Malley.

"In Patrick McGovern's ads and stump speeches, he talks about being raised by his single mother—Alice."

"Are you suggesting that Patrick McGovern's father was the captain of that boat shipping the illegal goods?"

"If he was, we might be looking at a conspiracy here!" said Cooper.

"We need to get over to the mayoral debate—STAT!" O'Malley jerked the steering wheel and spun the car around. "Hold on, Cooper." And with that, the detectives sped off into the night.

KALAMAZOO CITY UNIVERSITY, MAIN AUDITORIUM, 5:50 P.M.

Zengo arrived back in the dressing room just before Myers. McGovern was no longer there. Zengo had the satisfaction of asking "Where have you been?" when the manager rushed through the door.

"Just meeting with someone," said Myers. "And it paid off—I've got your debate curveball right here, Frank. McGovern, the 'man of the people,' has not been on the straight and narrow when it comes to his finances."

Pandini perked up his ears.

"The reason why he's been able to buy so much

airtime for his attack ads is because he's been receiving money from Nutter's Nuts. He's been running a pro-nut platform because he's getting paid to."

Myers held up his hand for a high five, but Pandini was deep in thought. "I don't know what you expect me to do with this information," he finally said.

Myers was shocked. "You've got to be kidding me, sir," he said.

"I don't know if I want to stoop to that level," said Pandini. "No matter how much I want to win this election, McGovern is an old friend. I'm not willing to embarrass him with hearsay. Once the press gets ahold of it, true or not, they'll print it everywhere."

Myers said, "Respectfully, sir, this is the only way. It's not as if everything McGovern has said about you is fair. It's time we punch back!"

"Not like this, Irving."

Zengo admired Pandini's principled stance and opened his bill to say so. But Myers cut him off.

"Shouldn't you be checking on security arrangements or something?" he snapped. "I don't think your career will survive another assault on Mr. Pandini."

Zengo sighed and left the room to give the stage a final sweep. He saw nothing out of the ordinary. He did see a fully packed auditorium. Not just with students and ordinary citizens, but with reporters as well. The reporters, in fact, seemed to have multiplied even just in the last day or so. He could hardly see anything but for the pulse of flashbulbs. And he could hardly hear anything but for the general hubbub.

Only when he had assured himself that Bobby and his team were manning security at all the doors did he relax his vigilance. He went back to the dressing room to check in.

Television reporter Jaiden Meltzer was moderating that evening's debate. He was shaking Pandini's hand when Zengo entered the room.

"Good luck tonight, Mr. Pandini."

"Thank you, Jaiden."

Zengo looked across the stage and saw Patrick McGovern buttoning up his suit coat. He looked confident, unfazed by all the commotion of the evening.

Meltzer made his way to shake McGovern's hand and then took his seat at the moderator's desk, placed before two podiums. A floor-to-ceiling photo of the Kalamazoo City skyline provided a backdrop. The house lights went down, and the crowd's murmur was reduced to a hush.

Meltzer smiled a wide grin and said, "Welcome, everyone, to the first debate in this special election for mayor of Kalamazoo City! Thank you for joining us this evening. First, let's welcome the candidates."

Pandini and McGovern walked to the center of the stage, shook hands, and took to their podiums.

Zengo and Myers stood just offstage. Zengo kept his eyes roving around the room. Myers still seemed nervous, but he was paying rapt attention at the same time.

Meltzer explained the rules. Each candidate would take turns being the first to answer a question, followed by a minute when the other candidate could answer. He began by asking Patrick McGovern: "How would you solve the city's current budget crisis?"

"Thank you for the opportunity to answer that fine question," said McGovern. "The real crisis our beloved city faces is one of confidence. Our citizens need a mayor they can trust, one whose character is above reproach and whose past is an open book. I am that candidate. My opponent is not. We need a public servant who puts the public first and business interests second. I am that candidate. My opponent is not. . . ."

As he went on and on, talking about how rich Pandini was, how out of touch with the common citizen, Zengo could see that Pandini was getting worked up.

Finally, Meltzer turned to Pandini. "Mr. Pandini, you have one minute to respond."

Before Pandini began to speak, Myers's cell phone rang again. He excused himself and disappeared. *Where is he going now?* wondered Zengo. Then he turned his attention to what Pandini was saying.

"I have met many fine citizens in the course of this campaign," began Pandini. "I know about their plight and their pain."

Across the stage, McGovern scoffed. Pandini must have noticed. He continued. "Mr. District Attorney, you say you are against businesses having a hand in city government. Yet your own campaign has been fueled by, and influenced by, a major corporate entity."

"That's rubbish, Mr. Pandini. It is you—"

Pandini raised his hand to silence McGovern. "It's not rubbish, sir. It's nuts. Quite literally. You have been taking an enormous amount of money from Nutter's Nuts. Which is why you oppose my stance on nuts. I'm sorry, Mr. McGovern, but isn't the safety of our students more important than your campaign funds?"

The crowd gasped. Jaiden Meltzer pleaded with the crowd to maintain their composure so that they could stay on schedule and abide by the strict guidelines set forth for debates.

McGovern was fumbling for just the right comeback. Across the auditorium, flashbulbs were popping. Pandini had nailed his opponent.

At that moment, the skylights above shattered, showering the crowd with broken glass.

A dozen masked flying squirrels swooped down onto the stage.

KALAMAZOO CITY UNIVERSITY, MAIN AUDITORIUM, 7:05 P.M.

Zengo withdrew his boomerang and charged the stage. "PLATYPUS POLICE SQUAD! FREEZE!" The detective stood center stage, placing himself between Pandini and the masked assailants. There were about a dozen of them. He could take down seven of them with his rapid-fire boomerang technique. He'd wrestle the remainder if he could catch them before they fled.

But when each masked squirrel withdrew a boomerang, Zengo knew the odds were not in his favor.

"I suggest you step aside," said the biggest,

scruffiest squirrel. He aimed his boomerang right at Zengo's head. "We're here for Pandini. We don't want any problems."

"Well, you've got a problem, punk," said Zengo, drawing himself up to his full height. He towered over the squirrel. "If you want Pandini, you'll need to go through me."

Jaiden Meltzer dove under the moderator's desk. Patrick McGovern ran backstage. Pandini remained at his podium with his head held high.

Zengo's pulse throbbed; he could feel the sweat trickle down his back. "I know where you're from. You're from Nutter's Nuts."

The squirrels looked at each other. *Who snitched?*

"Not only that," said Zengo. "I know you're not really flying squirrels."

"That's where you're wrong, Detective," said the scruffiest squirrel. He turned to his comrades. "ACTIVATE!" he called. Each squirrel clicked a button on a special wrist band. The flaps they had glided in on folded up and disappeared—and jets sprouted from special packs on their backs.

Zengo had to admit, it looked pretty cool.

"Now drop your weapon and get out of the way, or things are going to get really ugly around here," spat the ringleader.

"The Platypus Police Squad NEVER backs down!" shouted Zengo, keeping his boomerang locked on the ringleader of the group, who was aiming to launch a boomerang right at Zengo's head in return.

"You got that right!"

Jo Cooper was suddenly at his side. She held her boomerang locked on the gang. "Drop your weapons!"

"You mess with one of us, you mess with all of us," called O'Malley, who crept up from stage left with his boomerang at the ready. "We know who sent you. It's over."

One of the squirrels stepped forward. The crowd screamed as he turned and faced the auditorium, boomerang held at the ready. "Frank Pandini Jr.'s anti-nut legislation is a threat to the entire city! And he hasn't complied with our demands. Now we are taking matters into our own hands!"

Eight of the squirrels jumped on Pandini and grabbed hold of him. Their jetpacks burst to life and they lifted him up into the air above the crowd.

O'Malley aimed at the fleeing squirrels and pulled back to throw his boomerang. But before he could let it loose, another scurry of squirrels grabbed hold of him and lifted him up into the air too. Soon both captives were being carried out of the auditorium through the broken skylights.

"Quick! Let's go!" Zengo called to Cooper.

Cooper flashed her badge to the audience. "All of you—remain in your seats!"

The two detectives raced out of the building.

"Cooper," said Zengo breathlessly, "thanks for your help back there."

Cooper gave him a smile that might almost be called friendly. "I never leave a fellow detective hanging."

Once they spilled out into the street, they looked up at the night sky. The two groups of kidnappers flew in opposite directions, carrying their victims.

Zengo looked from Pandini to O'Malley and back again. Every second counted.

"You take the squad car. Go save O'Malley," he said. "I'll go after Pandini." As he ran after his set of squirrel perps, he called back, "Don't let them out of your sight, Cooper. And keep your radio on."

Zengo flashed his badge at a biker and said, "The

Platypus Police Squad needs to borrow your bike." Before he could respond, Zengo had pulled him off his motorcycle. "And your helmet. Safety first!"

Zengo buckled the helmet, gunned the engine, and roared off.

THE STREETS OF KALAMAZOO CITY, 7:15 P.M.

Zengo's fur blew straight back as he zoomed through the streets of Kalamazoo City. As he weaved through traffic, he never lost sight of the flying squirrels on the horizon. At every turn, cars swerved to avoid him, nearly clipping him several times. Drivers leaned on their horns and shook their fists. Zengo wished he had a siren, but the best he could do was drive on and hope his luck held.

He caught every green light until he got to Pandini Crossing, where the light changed just as he drew up. Should he stop? He scanned the darkening skies, glad for the light of the rising moon. The perps and their prisoner were almost out of sight. He opened the throttle and sped through the red light, narrowly missing an oncoming city bus.

An engine roared behind him. Glancing in the side mirror, he saw an enormous tractor trailer bearing down. Worse yet—there was a masked squirrel behind the wheel!

Zengo gripped the throttle tighter and accelerated again. He was determined not to lose sight of Pandini. But if he didn't get that truck off his tail, he was going to be roadkill. Another glance in his mirror told him the truck was gaining on him. Zengo had no choice.

He eyed the fast-approaching intersection. If he

swung wide enough to the left, his odds of clearing the turn at this speed were decent. He took a deep breath and braced himself.

Just then another eighteen-wheeler barreled down from that direction, pulled its brakes, and skidded sideways, blocking the road. Not only would Zengo not be able to turn left, he wouldn't be able to continue driving straight. The Nutter's Nuts logo was emblazoned on the side of the trailer.

Zengo didn't stop to think. He had to try his favorite trick from every awesome cop movie he had ever seen. He hoped it would work. He tilted the bike over

as far as possible, shut his eyes, and held his breath. If he could have taken his hands off the bars, he would have crossed his fingers, too.

The motorcycle skidded across the pavement underneath the truck, sending up sparks. Zengo's head was almost taken out by the underside of the truck. When he dared to open his eyes, he and the bike were safe on the other side. The bike skidded to a stop, and Zengo jumped off. His leg throbbed. He could barely stand. But he couldn't think about the pain right now. He had to get out of there.

He leaped to the side of the road, just in time. The trucks collided, sending up flames. Debris flew everywhere. Hunks of flaming metal fell on either side of him. He turned to look at the wreckage—it was a

disaster. He stopped to catch his breath.

And felt the cold steel of a boomerang, placed at his temple.

"Hands up!" said a rough voice. Zengo turned slowly to see the squirrel who had been in the truck behind him.

"Don't try anything stupid," came another voice from the darkness. It was the other truck driver.

Zengo was relieved that they hadn't been in the middle of that explosion, but he wasn't happy to be at boomerang-point while the kidnappers made their escape.

Zengo slowly reached his webbed hands to the sky, and at the same time got ready to pull his second-favorite cop trick. He reached for the goon's arm, pulled him in, and head-butted him, knocking him out. Then he swung the unconscious squirrel around and threw him into his accomplice, knocking him down too—and out. He grabbed the fallen squirrels by the collars and lifted them off their feet. He shook them awake.

"Where's the panda?"

"Okay, easy! He's on the roof of Nutter's Nut Factory."

Zengo looked down the road. The factory was a few miles away—by the time he got there, he didn't know what the squirrels would have done to Pandini.

A car barreled down the road, headed straight for Zengo. *Not again*, he thought as he was blinded by the headlights. The tires let out a deafening screech as the car came to a stop, just inches away from where Zengo stood.

"Hey, Rick—need a lift?" called O'Malley from the passenger seat.

"You did it!" Zengo shouted to Cooper, who was driving.

"Get in!" she yelled.

Zengo cuffed the squirrels and threw them in the backseat. He jumped in beside them and knocked on the plastic partition behind his partner's head. That's when he saw O'Malley's arm in a sling. "What happened?"

"Injured it when those squirrels dropped me," he said. "But I'll be all right. Cooper, step on it!"

NUTTER'S NUT FACTORY, 7:33 P.M.

Cooper slowly approached the factory, cutting the headlights. It was eerily quiet: no workers, no smoke, no movement at all. The plant typically ran on a twenty-four-hour operation to keep up with the demand. Something was going on.

They pulled up to the shipping dock and Cooper put the car in park. "Corey, you stay here in the car while Zengo and I go in."

"No way," said O'Malley, opening the door. "There's no way the two of you can take those squirrels on your own."

We need someone to be the lookout, and your arm is broken," she replied.

"Okay, fine! I'll radio for backup. But be careful."

Cooper and Zengo crept up to the factory wall. "What's the plan?" she whispered.

Zengo pointed to the roof. "They're up there."

"We can't just go up there boomerangs blazing," said Cooper. "They are armed—and dangerous."

Zengo shook his head. "Don't worry," he said, pulling out his phone and sending a text message. "We won't be alone."

The detectives pulled their boomerangs from their holsters. Zengo spotted a fire-escape ladder and pointed up. Cooper nodded. They double-checked that the coast was clear and signaled to O'Malley, who responded with a thumbs-up.

Zengo leaped to grab the lowest rung of the ladder. He pulled himself up, glad for all those hours in the gym. Cooper came right behind.

When they got near the top, Zengo's tail brushed past Cooper's nose. She stifled a sneeze. They both froze. Zengo's heart pounded. They would be easy targets if they were discovered. But no one approached the edge.

They pulled themselves up and onto the roof, then ducked behind a smokestack. They could see all of Kalamazoo City spread out around them, with Pandini Towers standing proud to the east, taller than all the rest.

There was a cluster of figures at the center of the roof. Pandini sat in a chair, his arms tied behind his back, disheveled but apparently unharmed.

A shadowy figure with a shock of white hair stood before Pandini, his back toward Zengo and Cooper.

"So, Pandini," said a deep voice. "It has come to this. You want to bring down Nutter's Nuts. I won't have it."

Zengo recognized that voice—he'd been hearing it in television commercials since he was a kid. The shock of white hair was unmistakable.

It was Mr. Nutter.

"Jacob, this is pointless," said Pandini. "You're not a kidnapper. What do you think you're doing? We are friends."

"Friends don't destroy each other's businesses, Frank," said Nutter. "Your campaign stops here."

The squirrels flanking Pandini crept closer to him, but before any of them could lay a finger on the panda, Zengo and Cooper came charging.

"Platypus Police Squad! Hands in the air!" yelled Zengo. The squirrels turned and threw their boomerangs at the charging detectives. Zengo and Cooper jumped in separate directions and rolled behind stacks of crates. The squirrels leaped into the air, fired up their jetpacks, and launched more boomerangs from above.

The crate in front of Zengo shattered into a thousand pieces. He spun around to flee and called for Cooper. "Aim for their packs! We don't want any casualties!"

Zengo threw his boomerang over his shoulder. It was a direct hit. The jets sputtered and the squirrel did a face-plant onto the roof. Zengo caught his boomerang as another squirrel shot at his feet. Zengo sidestepped and chucked his boomerang and again—another precise hit.

Cooper threw round after round as well, taking out each of the jetpacks in rapid fire. Zengo had never seen anything like it.

Still, they were outnumbered—and the team of attackers grew as squirrels rushed up onto the roof from inside the building. Every one of them was armed. They circled Zengo and Cooper and began to close in.

"Whatever happens here," said Cooper, "it's been a pleasure working alongside you. You're as good a detective as O'Malley says you are."

"It's not over yet, Cooper," said Zengo, looking up.

A whoosh of wind came from above, and a moment later a sleek helicopter hovered over the roof.

"Let's even up these odds a bit, shall we?" said Bobby over the chopper's speaker. Pandini's entire security squad descended onto the scene. Bobby threw on a spotlight, temporarily blinding the squirrels.

"Put your hands in the air where I can see them!" Zengo shouted. The squirrels all dropped their boomerangs, each landing with a clang, and slowly raised their hands. Soon, they were all in handcuffs.

Zengo stepped up to Nutter. "Did you really think that you'd get away with this?"

"I had no choice," said Mr. Nutter. "If Pandini won this election and his nut allergy legislation went through, my family's business was done for!"

"I don't believe you came up with this entire scheme on your own," said Cooper. "Organizing those attacks would have taken more resources and access than you had at your disposal. You had help from someone else—someone close to Mr. Pandini."

Nutter nodded sadly.

Cooper picked up her radio. "Bring him up, boys." She smiled at Zengo as they heard the sound of distant sirens growing closer.

Diaz and Lucinni came up onto the roof through the stairwell, escorting a fuming Patrick McGovern, with Corey O'Malley right behind them. McGovern was struggling in their grips. "Unhand me! What am I doing here? Frank? What is the meaning of this?"

"Do you want to tell us, Mr. Nutter?" Cooper asked.

"McGovern knew that Pandini was going to launch a campaign against nuts in Kalamazoo City," Nutter said, his head hanging low. "He approached me and promised he'd kill any anti-nut legislation if I got Pandini to drop out of the race."

“It’s a lie!” shouted McGovern. “I never! This is preposterous! Why would I do something like that?”

“Revenge,” said Cooper. “Pure and simple. Revenge for what Frank’s father did to your father the night he was arrested.”

“Well, I . . .” McGovern stammered. “It’s true, my father went to prison that night, but Frank’s been a friend to me since we were little. . . . Frank, please, tell me you don’t believe this nonsense!”

Pandini, now untied, looked his friend in the eye. “I don’t want to believe it, Pat. But ever since this campaign began, I have felt like I did not know my old

friend anymore. Then when you started those hateful attack ads, I truly did not know what to think."

Lucinni turned McGovern around, and Diaz slapped handcuffs on him. McGovern's head dropped low.

That's when Zengo turned around and noticed a familiar face at the doorway, jotting down notes in his notepad. It was Derek Dougherty, who was soon joined by a mob of reporters. They swarmed onto the roof, flashbulbs firing.

O'Malley swung around to Diaz and Lucinni. "Who tipped off these parasites?"

Diaz and Lucinni looked embarrassed. Each one tried to point at the other, and then they just shrugged.

O'Malley towered over Derek. "You and the other creeps better get out of here the way you came . . . or I will send you all back down via the shortcut!" He indicated the edge of the roof.

"Don't get your tail all tied up in a knot, Detective," said Derek, leading all the other reporters back to the stairs. "We'll be in touch later—for follow-ups."

"Swarming little gnats," growled O'Malley.

"Diaz and Lucinni, let's get these perps down to headquarters," said Cooper, indicating the shamed squirrels and the devastated McGovern. They made their way toward the rooftop-access door.

Pandini approached Zengo and O'Malley and held out a hand to Zengo. "Thank you for all your help, Detective. I owe you my life. And more than once, I might add."

Zengo returned his handshake. "It's been an honor, sir."

Pandini continued. "I think I am safe from further harm. And from a loss in the election, it would seem. I don't believe my opponent will be able to continue his campaign after all that has happened. As far as I'm concerned, it's time for you to return to your regular duties—with my eternal gratitude."

Zengo bowed his head. O'Malley clapped him on the shoulder. "We'll all be glad to have him back at headquarters," he said. The two old partners exchanged a smile.

Kalamazoo City Krier
HERO DETECTIVES
UNCOVER ELECTION
SCAND

PLATYPUS POLICE SQUAD HEADQUARTERS, 9:15 A.M.

Rick Zengo sat at his desk, happily poring over the latest *Kalamazoo City Krier.* Corey O'Malley sat at the next desk, looking at the same newspaper with considerably less enthusiasm. The headline splayed across each front page read HERO DETECTIVES UNCOVER ELECTION SCANDAL. The photo accompanying the article featured Zengo, Cooper, and O'Malley surrounded by the squirrels, a shamed Patrick McGovern, and a grateful Frank Pandini.

"What do you think?" said Zengo. "Not exactly my best side."

"No, not really. It's a photo of your face," said O'Malley. "If I had to choose your better side, it would be the back of your head."

"There's no such thing as bad publicity, though."

"This type of thing is just a distraction."

"You wouldn't be saying that because Derek spelled your name 'Korry O'Malley,' would you?"

"Hmmph," was all O'Malley said.

Cooper and Plazinski walked out from the sergeant's office. O'Malley and Zengo stood up. "Jo!" said Zengo. "Say it ain't so!"

"We can't stand to see you go!" said O'Malley. "Hey! That rhymed!"

"What are you talking about?" said Plazinski.

"We figured she was going back to Atlantis City," said Zengo.

"Now that the case is closed," said O'Malley.

"Not that we want her to," they both said.

Zengo punched O'Malley in the shoulder. "Jinx. You owe me a soda."

"Nope," said Cooper. "I'm staying right here. Besides," she added, "I think we make a pretty good team!"

The three detectives smiled at each other.

Even Plazinski agreed. "I got to admit," he said, "it took all three of you to bust this case up—can't see any point in breaking you up now. You're on a roll."

"Are you ready to head over to Frank's Franks and settle our bet?" said Cooper to Plazinski.

"No time like the present," said Plazinski, grinning grumpily in spite of himself.

"What's this about a bet?" said O'Malley.

"Plazinski bet me a footlong that after Zengo peeled off to work with Pandini, you guys would never want to work together again," said Cooper.

Zengo and O'Malley looked at each other.

Plazinski was a little embarrassed. "I can see I was wrong."

"See ya around, boys," said Cooper as she and

Plazinski headed out of the station.

O'Malley and Zengo sat back down at their desks. They folded up the newspapers, silence hanging between them.

O'Malley spoke up first. "I don't know if I ever told you how much your grandfather meant to me," he said. "He was a mentor, sure. But he was more than that. He was a friend, too. And that's all I've ever wanted to be to you, Rick."

Zengo rubbed his eye, which suddenly felt like it had something caught in it. "I'm lucky to work with you," he said. "That's what I was thinking when I was watching Pandini and McGovern's friendship fall apart. When I was just starting, I thought the only thing that mattered was taking charge, being a hero. I didn't understand that the only way to become the best was to team up with the best."

They smiled.

"I gotta ask you one question, though," said O'Malley.

"What's up?" said Zengo.

"I have to admit, I was a little hurt when you went to rescue Pandini instead of me. What was that all about?"

"Are you kidding?" said Zengo. "You really would have wanted me throwing boomerangs at the squirrels carrying you, trying to knock them out of the sky? I told Cooper to go after you because I trust her more than I trust myself. Have you ever seen that platypus throw a boomerang? But I swear, if you tell her I said that, I'll deny it!"

O'Malley laughed. "I have a feeling with Frank Pandini about to be crowned as mayor, we're going to have our work cut out for us."

"Truth," said Detective Rick Zengo.

PANDINI TOWERS, 9:45 A.M.

Pandini hung up his phone. He looked at Bobby and Irving Myers. "McGovern has officially dropped out of the race," he said, and tapped the newspaper lying open in front of him. "An investigation is still pending, but the damage has been done." In spite of this welcome news, his face was serious.

"Congratulations, boss!" said Bobby, clapping Pandini on the shoulder—his good shoulder.

Pandini smiled. But there was a trace of sadness in the smile.

Myers, however, could not contain his glee. "I have

to admit, I never thought your plan would work."

Pandini glanced up, his face an unreadable mask.

Myers, oblivious to his boss's expression—or the lack of one—continued. "Frame McGovern for the attacks? And bring in a real member of the PPS for your 'protection,' to make it all look legit? Pure genius."

"I hated to do it to Pat, I really did," said Pandini. "McGovern was my oldest friend. But he had the nerve to try to stand between me and the mayor's office, and I had no choice. Pat had to pay the price."

"And he did," said Myers.

"Bobby, I'd like you to reach out to your contacts in the penitentiary, get a message to Jacob Nutter for me," Pandini continued. "Reassure him that I'm going to be taking care of A.J. and the rest of his family just as soon as I take the oath of office. I won't forget what he's done for me."

"Okay, I'll get on that right away," said Bobby.

"Anything else, *Mayor* Pandini?" asked Myers.

"That's it for now, boys. And—thanks." Pandini stood up and clapped his closest comrades on the shoulder. They bustled out of the office.

The next mayor of Kalamazoo City was now alone with his thoughts—and with the dramatic view of the city that he had personally restored from a disaster to a triumph. On his way over to the windows, he stopped to gaze at a small framed photograph on his wall. It was a picture of him and his father, long before his father's arrest, when he was just a cub, leaving a Kalamazoo City Pirates ball game.

Pandini studied the photograph. "I promise to do you proud," he said aloud to his father. "They'll pay for what they've done."

He gazed out the window, thinking of the past, and the future.

ACKNOWLEDGMENTS

To Jordan Brown, thank you for hitting the middle grade beat with me once again! I am eternally grateful for the support from Debbie Kovacs, Randy Testa, Noel Barlow, and everyone at Walden Pond Press. Thank you to Caroline Sun, Jenna Lisanti, Katie Fitch, Bethany Reis, and everyone at HarperCollins; it is an honor to partner up with such a talented team! Thank you to Rebecca Sherman, Eddie Gamarra, and Deb Shapiro, for making up my squad.

Thank you to my real-world cop friends Corey McGrath and Chris Zengo, who continue to keep their communities safe and field all of my questions. For the 1998 Yellow Platypus at the Hole in the Wall Gang

Camp, my first instance of drawing a monotreme.

Thank you to Joey Weiser and Michele Chidester for their help in shading the art in this book! And a shout to Austin Gifford and Sylvia Peterson for keeping things running in my studio.

Most importantly, thank you to my girls—Gina, Zoe, and Lucy—for their constant and unparalleled support and patience. And yes, for Ralph, too. I'm sorry this book series isn't called Pug Police Squad.

JARRETT J. KROSOCZKA

is the author and illustrator of the Lunch Lady graphic novel series, a two-time winner of the Children's Choice Book Award, as well as many picture books. He can be heard on "The Book Report with JJK," his radio segment on SiriusXM's Kids Place Live. Jarrett lives in Northampton, Massachusetts, with his wife, two daughters, and their pug, Ralph Macchio. You can visit him online at www.studiojjk.com.

Also available as an ebook.

The Platypus Police Squad will return in . . .

PLATYPUS POLICE SQUAD:
NEVER SAY NARWHAL

Frank Pandini Jr. is mayor of Kalamazoo City, and billboards across town say "Your City—Better!" With crime at an all-time high, however, KC has been anything but. Detectives Zengo, O'Malley, and Cooper—on their own, with no one left to trust—soon begin to suspect that the trail of tyranny will lead them to the doorstep of a very powerful city official.